John Morey

Author of ROSE: The Missing Years

Finding Rose

'Love should never be this hard'

Finding Rose
A novel by John Morey

© 2020 John Morey

First published in Great Britain 2020

Acknowledgements:

Cover design: Gomango Creative

Copy editing: Jane Morey

For feedback, visit New Novel

Prologue

A chance meeting in Plymouth

It was the ring on her right hand he recognised first. She reached across to pick the apple from the stall, putting it in the bag she held in her left hand. Late Saturday afternoon at Plymouth Market was the best time to buy. He was second in the queue behind her.

She turned to face him, "John?" His eyes switched from the delicate hand to the direction of the voice – a voice he recognised with its mixture of Irish and Midlands dialect.

"It's me. Rose." Her eyes were fixed on his, smiling. That long lost feeling in the pit of his stomach returned.

His mind raced back to the time they were last together. The smell of woodsmoke; the gypsy campfire; her dark mysterious gaze. He remembered the moment their eyes first met. She was beautiful even then, at sixteen.

The emotional turmoil of that summer - seven years ago - swept over him once more.

CHAPTER ONE

How it all started - growing up in a small Leicestershire village seven years earlier

He had been a mere fifteen year old, cycling to school along the Leicestershire lanes, riding home with his best pal, Melv. They were special days. Later on he would depend on him a lot.

Their normal route took them through South Wigston park, out past a biscuit factory with it's sweet aroma filling the air, and the Premier Drum factory not far from the canal. These were good times for the local drum kit company. Rock and roll had really taken off. To cap it all Ringo Starr, drummer of The Beatles, played Premier. A priceless endorsement.

The local canal – or "cut" as it was called - rarely held much interest unless it happened to be frozen over. Not now, of course, because it was early summer, but John could not resist reminding Melv of one particular event earlier that year. He taunted him with, "Fancy a swim?" Joking of course. Melv knew what he meant but was keen to forget that cold winter afternoon.

That February had been particularly cold. Roads were gritted and pretty safe, but canals had frozen over for the second day running. "Let's see if we can walk across." He couldn't remember whose idea that was.

Neither shrank from the challenge. With bikes resting against the bridge they took precarious steps down to the tow path to the water's edge. "You go first," said Melv, "seeing that you're older." The ice *looked* safe. There was only one way to find out.

John tested the surface by tossing a rock into the middle. Good. The ice held, the rock spinning and sliding to the opposite bank. He placed his first tentative steps into the unknown.

There was a heart-stopping creak at first, but the ice closest to the bank still managed to bear John's light frame. "No stopping now," he thought, less confident as the fear of an ice-cold bath became a real possibility. He continued, shuffling across in small steps - a further attempt to reduce his impact on the fragile surface. The opposite side was only a few feet away. He paused, then using his favoured right leg to launch himself, he took a giant leap. To his relief his leg did not slip under him and he found firm ground with his left. "Your turn now."

"I told you the ice was thick enough." More sure of himself, Melv ventured out to follow his friend. Ice was thick enough in the middle, but he was just within a foot of the opposite bank and safety - when the ice gave way. Thankfully the water only came up to his waist. Smothering the need to laugh out loud John reached in to help him out. Melv was not happy. Soaking wet and freezing was one thing; explaining it to his Mum was another.

"Why didn't you tell me the ice was thin there?"

"You didn't ask."

John was about to give a longer more scientific answer. First, it was mainly down to weight – Melv was heavier than John. He found that funny – justice at last. Melv's Mum had always chided John because he was smaller and skinnier than her son. It was almost as if to say, 'Don't your parents feed you?' He resented her remarks. Now it was payback time. 'Thin is "in"', he thought. Second, and something he had recently learned in physics, Melv hadn't realised water next to the bank is ever so slightly warmer than that in the middle, and therefore weaker.

But that was now history – or rather science – and did not address the current problem: How to get Melv's trousers dry between now and reaching home, only twenty minutes ride away.

"You'd better come back to my place." suggested John. That would at least buy them time.

It was just getting dark, and he noticed that a light was on. "Unusual," he thought. His Mum normally left work at 5 o'clock. She was early that day. "We're in luck Melv. You can dry yourself in front of the fire. Mum might even iron your trousers."

7

John led Melv straight into the front room, then went back into the kitchen to tell his Mum about their accident. Taking off his trousers, Melv held them in front of the roasting open fire. He was careful not to get them too close otherwise the Terylene material might scorch, or even melt! He also warmed himself. Meanwhile John's Mum made them both a jam sandwich. (One each!) Dry, then ironed, the trousers were returned to their rightful owner. He welcomed the warm material against his legs as he put them back on. Melv was good to go.

John had never thought much of it before, but the fact that Melv's trousers were made of Terylene meant they hardly lost their crease. Even when wet. He compared that with his own, cheaper trousers made of a wool-based material. He felt a twinge of envy – embarrassment I suppose – because it showed how Melv's parents must have been a bit more better-off than his. Melv's Mum obviously thought this, given the jibes she made about him not being fed properly.

Later on when he was lying awake in bed he returned to these thoughts, leaving him feeling just a little bit sorry for his parents. Then he recalled all the good things they did for him, all the kindness they lavished on his brother and sisters as well as on him. It was the little things.

He remembered the Wagon Wheels chocolate biscuits she had put in his lunch at primary school – a real treat. And the new comic she bought him one time – the first edition and one that other kids hadn't heard of. Best of all he could hardly forget the time she took him to buy a new coat for school.

Normally she would buy a blue gaberdine mac, it was school uniform and not too expensive. On this occasion they were in Leicester when John happened to see a camel coloured overcoat in the window of a shop they were passing. It wasn't the normal shop for uniforms but John begged her to let him try it on. The shop assistant found his size. It fitted perfectly and he really looked the part – raglan sleeves and all! He wanted that coat.

Then came the price. John could see the look of surprise on his Mum's face, which turned into a look of disappointment on his own. It was more than she could afford – but he really,

really *did* want that coat. She asked him to wait outside while she talked it over with the assistant. John noticed the to-and-fro shaking of heads before there was a final nod – from the shop assistant.

It was less than the ticket price and it took every penny his Mum had, leaving just enough for the bus fares home. Only then did he understand how selfish he had been, making his Mum go without other things just, so that he could have his precious coat, but later he loved his Mum all the more. As he did right now, thinking back. He hardly noticed the one tear that had fallen onto his pillow as he fell asleep – full of so much love for his Mum and Dad.

On the way home from school the next day, John learnt that Melv did not escape without *some* flack from his own mother. 'Why was he so late back from school.' Typical Melv and not to be outdone he turned the tables back on his mother, reminding her he *had* told her that *very* morning he was going to John's for tea. Of course, it was a total lie, but he still paid for it. Unfortunately, as he had already eaten he had to forgo his proper tea, making do with the solitary jam sandwich at John's!

He had just finished the story yet again – 'rubbing it in' Melv called it – when they arrived at the ford leading up to Gypsy Lane. They often took the back lane where it left the main road from Wigston. It was a short-cut to their village of Blaby.

Crossing the ford was either fun or fiasco depending on the height of the water. Today it was low so they chanced cycling across. They took a run at it, lifting their legs up as high as they could, and forward, while the water splayed outwards from the wheels. They crossed one behind the other so as not to splash each other.

It led to Mill Lane – the official name for Gypsy Lane. Gypsies favoured it because it was quiet and convenient for the village. It was also next to a water supply and, with a farm nearby for fresh milk and eggs, it provided essentials. And sometimes work.

You often hear stories of gypsies being at odds with local

villagers, farmers in particular. In this case you could call it a peaceful coexistence. Quite often the local farmer needed extra hands during harvesting or at lambing time. He knew that Romany people understood the countryside much more than his village neighbours. They didn't need to be told what to do, or how to do it. Basic skills and knowledge were passed down over the generations, just like the farming way of life.

Grazing for their ponies was a broad grass verge. With open fields and woodland nearby, this meant additional sources of food for the gypsies, after dark of course. The taking of rabbits, the odd pheasant or partridge, and firewood, was tolerated by the farmer. Sometimes their knowledge of animals even saved him vet's bills. Horses were an important form of transport in post-war days, for farmers as well as gypsies. The Romany family that John and Melv cycled past had two ponies: one for the caravan (or "vardo"); the smaller one for the trap.

The boys would often launch into the latest pop song as they cycled – hands-free – weaving side to side down the traffic free country lanes. John's yellow Dawes Domino would glide silently in middle gear, whilst Melv's Raleigh gave an irritating "clank". Its chain guard caught the frame at each turn. Some would say it helped them to keep time. Others could do without it. For one thing, singing helped the journey go quicker. It became a little tedious some days taking the same route with nothing ever happening. But that was about to change.

On this occasion John was cycling head in the air in full voice. Melv was building in the harmonies. They were especially keen on The Hollies and The Everly Brothers, with secret ambitions to be like them one day. Suddenly there was a scream and "Look out!" bringing him to his senses, and crashing to the ground. Instinctively he had swerved to avoid the figure in front of him.

"What was that?" he moaned, holding his bleeding left knee. He slowly got to his feet only to see 'the figure' disappear into the caravan. His first reaction was to follow, but immediately his dad's words came to him, "You leave them alone, and they'll leave you alone." He was referring to gypsies in general. So he did.

"You OK?"

"Sort of," said John, "but who was that? Are they hurt?"

"Doubt it, seeing as how quickly they scarpered. It was a 'she', anyway."

That was pretty much that. Apart from cuts and bruises and a bent spoke or two and torn trousers, he was OK. How would he explain that? Not with, 'Look mam. No hands!' John thought he'd leave that bit out. New trousers were expensive, even cheap ones! His Mum would end up patching them.

That would serve him right.

Cycling to school in the mornings was different. He rarely met up with Melv and only ever saw an old lady in the gypsy camp. The main reason, he learnt later, was that the head Romany's wife used the pony and trap to take the children to the local primary school after dropping her husband off at the site where he worked. They were widening the main Lutterworth Road through Blaby and beyond, towards Lutterworth, in fact.

Gypsies' skills on the tarmac were well sought after. When one section of road was completed they broke camp, following the road gang as it worked on this major route all the way to London. They were all used to an ever-changing life, especially the three children. They had become reliant on each other, self-sufficient and hardly missing the companionship of permanent school friends. Come late afternoon they were home, leaving school earlier than them.

The eldest – daughter – found casual work at the local farm just a short walk up on Mill Lane. She was home early each afternoon, or that was John's hope. Based on the few furtive glances they had shared it was clear that she was so beautiful. She was slim, tanned and had a wholesome 'outdoors' look about her that attracted him. It was stark contrast to some of the girls at school who could be pale and sickly, or caked in make-up.

As soon as he was in sight of the camp John subconsciously began to cycle more slowly. He might even dismount, making excuses that his chain needed checking, purely to increase the chances of seeing her. Or, as he imagined, it might give her a better chance to find *her* own excuses and just happen to be there at the side of the road or busying herself by the camp fire when he passed. If they saw each other neither spoke, but he convinced himself that she had almost smiled at him once, not with her mouth but with those dazzling eyes. It was there, but gone in a second. And it stayed with him.

The younger children must have been twins; a boy and a girl around ten years old. His gypsy girl he guessed would have been around fifteen or sixteen, but surprisingly shy. Shy or not, she became John's one dream in his quieter moments. He could not tell even Melv. With Romany black hair and delicate features she was just blossoming into womanhood. Even those stolen glances as John cycled past revealed eyes with an unsettling mystical quality. They bore straight into John, into his very being. She wanted him too.

CHAPTER TWO
John receives a Romany blessing

Several days after John's spill the boys had cause to stop at the camp once more. Initially it was curiosity, drawn by the collection of people gathered round a heap - but they couldn't determine what - on the grass verge.

John saw the mother comforting the twins, clearly in some distress. The father was pacing up and down in a state of agitation. Even the farmer had raced across his fields at the commotion. He was still out of breath. Just arriving by bike was the local Bobby, Mr Madison. But John was puzzled to see the doctor's car.

It was one of the few cars in the village of that size so he was not surprised to recognise Dr. Drury. He was crouching over the 'heap' on the grass verge. He later understood why. Unable to find the vet they had summoned the doctor. He had a car and his surgery was less than a quarter of a mile away. But the ailing patient turned out to be Jessie - the gypsies' pony that pulled the vardo.

Both dropped their cycles and walked closer to the gathering. The poor creature was breathing in slow, deep breaths, exhaling heavily through his nostrils. She was on her side, her eyes overly wide trying to take in all those around her. Barely able to flick the occasional annoying fly from its ears, the pony's eyes told the true story. Jessie knew she was dying.

With a look of fear the old mare was still clearly conscious, but showing a sense of bewilderment. What was happening to her? Who were all these people? What was all the fuss about? Where was Rose....? Dr. Drury had seen that look before in humans. He sent a signal to the father as soon as he could catch his eye, to prepare him for the worst. Melv, meanwhile, had walked over to where the mother was comforting her youngest. He tried to add his support but even he was struggling to find the right words.

John, on the other hand, was transfixed. Although caught up in the tragic event, he was strangely perplexed as to *why* he was so moved. Why was he so saddened by the plight of an animal he only knew by sight? He felt he had to be there – but why? And he simply could not look down in case the pony saw him looking, had caught *his* eye, and would expect him to help her. All he could do was stare out across the fields to the old mill in the distance, he needed to do just that – nothing else - powerless to do anything. Without really being aware of his own state, he was caught in a trance as an aura descended onto and around him. He barely noticed the sobs and inaudible sympathies from those who had now created an even closer circle. Watching. Waiting.

Without warning a strange sense of calm and inner warmth engulfed him, comforting him. Someone's hand – smaller, softer and finer – caught hold of his. It was the beautiful gypsy girl. Almost as if responding to a signal, at that very moment the mare emitted a long groan from deep down as her final breath left her body. The very instant the mare breathed her last, releasing her final grasp on life, he was gripped by a feeling he had never experienced before. Some benign power from the dying pony coursed through his body. Then the hand that had held his so softly tightened until he was almost sure he would cry out. He opened his mouth, caught his breath, but no sound would come.

The gypsy girl, he had found out was called Rose, had finally conquered her shyness to share the moment with him. He was the only one who could carry her through this moment. To make sense of it. For what reason he did not know. Nor did he care; nor did it matter. What was happening to them was not apparent to those around them, but it was no less real nor less powerful. Rose and John continued to gaze into the far distance as the silence around them intensified. After several minutes sound, movement, and grief took over and filled to void. It was the dark before the dawn; the quiet before the storm. Now no-one spoke other than in a whisper. John and Rose would not have heard in any case. They were only aware of each other and the bond forming between them.

Her hand squeezed his a second time before she broke their silence, "Come on." Still in a daze he followed her as she weaved her way through the gathering which was gradually starting to disperse, leaving the family to recover quietly and in privacy.

To resist her would have been pointless. With a final 'Goodbye' to her beloved Jessie and letting go of his hand she led him through the gate, across the meadow and towards the stream. Only then did she turn to face him. She was certain he would be standing before her. "Thank you."

"She's at peace now," he said.

"I know. I felt it. So did you."

"How do you know?"

"Jessie has given us a bond. She felt your spirit. She joined ours."

"Why are you so sure -?" John paused. He was unsettled. Uneasy. He could do nothing but stand there, looking at her beautiful serene face, drowning in her eyes.

She answered simply, "The days you would cycle past? When Jessie and I were at the camp? Waiting? She would breath - almost a sigh - through her nostrils as soon as she heard you approach. She was letting me know that you and I would be bonded. She wanted it. It was she who pushed me into your path a few days ago when you fell off your bike. It was her way. Jessie knew I would need something – someone – when she passed away. And she was aware of how little time she had for this life."

"Sorry," she added.

Throughout all this her eyes never left John's, searching for signs that he was taking it all in, understanding it all. Gradually her eyes deepened, glistening as her grief surfaced, but she kept it in control. Barely.

"Sorry, Rose."

"You know my name?"

"Yes. I heard your sister call to you a while back. She certainly wasn't shouting like that at your mother. Or your Gran."

They both smiled, partly out of relief, partly because they knew this was the beginning of a new closeness. Yes, a friendship was forming, and their need for each other was finally out in the open.

John was still overwhelmed but determined to search for more answers. "What you said about our bonding? What did you mean? How did you know...why?"

She knew she owed him an explanation. "We have certain beliefs in Romany lore, handed down over centuries. Those we care about, rely upon and believe in – whether people or animals – have a power. They have the will to pass on their love when they die. Usually it is one-to-one; on rare occasions this can also bind *two* people. Jessie chose both you *and* me to receive her gift.

Come, let's sit down and think about what has just happened. I know it must be strange for you. I need to take it in as well. We don't need to talk. Let's just enjoy the gift." She seemed so adult.

They sat down by the stream, gradually their senses returning to the soft sounds of the world around them. Distant purring of the tractor two fields away; the meadow larks in full song, announcing the new spring; and the gurgling of the cool waters next to them as it meandered carefree downstream - all combined to bring them slowly back to reality. They sat in silence. Listening. Healing. But not mourning. It could even have been a celebration, but a solemn one.

Eventually and instinctively they joined hands. The spiritual aura returned to wash through their bodies. It overpowered all their other senses apart from sight and touch. Pure calm, wholeness and completeness consumed them.

"Jessie will always be with us," she whispered, her hand reaching up to caress his cheek. "And you will always be with me."

CHAPTER THREE

A Romany summer – the perfect gift

Rose and John shared the gift from that day onwards. It was a secret between them. Those around them also *felt* a change in them, saw glimpses of their unspoken bond. Rose's parents witnessed a transformation normally only found in Romany families, when a girl from one camp forms attachment to a boy from another. But they accepted it. They accepted him.

They liked John and didn't interfere, even though he would spend the whole day - alone - with their daughter who was already promised to another. One day. Right now it was the last thing Rose wanted to think about. She knew she had found the right one, or rather Jessie had – *for* her. Her soul mate. Even though she knew nothing about him, had hardly heard him speak, she 'felt' him.

Rose's only duty was to the gift bestowed upon them by Jessie. It cancelled out all other betrothals. John was now her chosen one and it was to him she focused all her devotion. John would return that in equal measure. She was sure of that. Every moment they spent together would draw them closer. If Rose revealed to him the secrets and properties of plants and herbs in field and hedgerow, he in turn would explain the significance of the stars and planets – the knowledge he had learnt in his science class. That was the way they connected, but it was 'how' they conveyed that connection to each other that bound them.

John's passion for poetry and literature fascinated her. Her own schooling was scant at best and disjointed. Lessons were rarely about serious subjects such as sciences and general knowledge; but sewing and cooking. She had never heard the words of Robert Frost or Gerard Manley Hopkins until he spoke them. But it was how he spoke them that she listened to and that's what touched her most. It was one of his gifts to her. Others' words now conveyed the depths of his feelings for her. Not that he could remember poems and stories by heart. He would leave her with literary collections so that she could read them if he wasn't there. But when she was reading them alone they only made sense if she imagined his voice speaking the words on the pages, as if they were his words. *His* thoughts.

John Steinbeck was his favourite author and soon became hers. Rose was amazed that there could even *be* such a place as California, let alone the kind of people that he depicted in Cannery Row and Monterey. They were so different from any she had ever seen or met. And one word in *East of Eden* intrigued her, 'timshel'. It was a Mandarin word that roughly translated meant 'Thou mayest'. It fitted how she felt about their own destiny. It was like the legacy left to them by Jessie. It described the gift bestowed on them to follow their own destiny and their own dreams. As one.

The best days were when John was allowed free periods from school. He could spend precious time with her when she wasn't working at the farm. He was excused from attending classes and could revise *with* Rose. He would take his set books and she would ask him questions, checking his answers. On those days they would take Bess, his collie cross. She had been 'his' ever since she was fetched from kennels on the lap of his eldest sister – whilst she rode pillion behind her boyfriend on his motorbike! Bess was always travel sick after that. She was now twelve years old. Over the years she had become his one soul mate, going everywhere with him on his walks in the countryside – before he met Rose.

He used to laugh when Rose teased Bess. He and Rose would be sat in a field leaning back to back against each other, John revising, Rose gave out answers. Bess would be close to them, ecstatic while Rose gently played with the collie's ears. Then Rose would suddenly stop and take her hand away - and wait - wondering how long it would be before Bess' paw would reach out to touch her shoulder as if to say, 'Don't stop now.' Sometimes, if they sat close to the hedgerow in a field, and if they were quiet and patient a rabbit might appear from it's burrow, nose twitching and looking round until, spotting them just feet away, it would bolt back in for safety. Bess rarely noticed. If it was a ploughed field not yet grassed over they would sit watching flocks of lapwing – 'pee-wits' they called them – grazing. During nesting season he would often watch them land but – up until now - he was never able to find their nests. Rose changed all that - one of many secrets she shared.

His own parents too welcomed the 'new John'. During his early teenage years they would lose patience coping with his fractious behaviour and mild tantrums when they might ask him to do the washing up after tea or other household chores. Now he seemed so helpful, never once complaining if asked to mow the lawn or fetch a loaf from the shops – or even tidy his room!. They knew about Rose but he rarely invited her home to see them. 'Typical,' his Mum would say to herself.' Find a girl and forget about your dear old Mum overnight.' But they did approve. Before moving into the village itself they had lived on their smallholding just outside. He remembered his dad actually being glad of the gypsies – as well as students – who he could employ on a day basis for pea-picking. Whole families would turn up and he would pay them by the bushel load. They worked hard, in turn he learned to respect them.

Now that Rose was on the scene John was often ribbed by his friends for being absent from their soccer and cricket games after school and at weekends. He was now totally with Rose of course and knew things about girls that they didn't. 'They'll soon learn,' he thought, but he doubted they would ever experience the unique world that he and Rose had created for themselves. She marvelled at what he knew about building bridges and dams, and foreign countries (from his geography lesson) – plus all about kings and queens of the past.

Likewise, he was fascinated to learn all she knew about nature and the countryside, plants and animals. One of their favourite pastimes was fishing for brook trout just downstream from the ford, at the bottom of Mill Lane. Occasionally they were lucky enough to take a couple back for supper at the camp. That was a real treat, especially the way Mrs Lee, Rose's Mum, cooked them with herbs and secret ingredients that only she knew. For 'afters' occasionally they would have wild 'pig nuts' – foraged by Rose's brother and sister where they were growing in places only they were able to find. John didn't know such delicacies existed. They were delicious.

Over the weeks and months, the young couple's spiritual oneness grew into a deeper physical attraction, adding to the secret world to which they retreated when the need took them. Their devotion became more intense as the summer wore on. It was the first experience of its kind for both of them, and they made their discoveries without interference or guidance from anyone else. Rose's Mum had passed on some cautionary advice. John received similar advice from his school biology lessons, but on the emotional level they found their own instincts served them best. It was on the same plain as the height and depth of feelings as they had felt on the first day they had found each other – the day that Jessie bestowed on them her gift.

The same 'rush' swept over him as he found himself staring into Rose's eyes seven years later, in Plymouth Market.

CHAPTER FOUR

Rose has disappeared - John goes to Southampton to study

His Mum and Dad were moving to the Isle of Wight where his oldest sister and family already ran a guest house. He was accepted on a diploma course in Southampton which suited his parents who wanted him to be near. There were no similar courses in Leicester. But there was still Rose to consider. Or so he thought...

It was during the few days he was away in Southampton for interviews that he later discovered Rose and her family broke camp in Blaby to move away. He found a note pushed through his door on his return, saying she had to go back to Ireland with her parents. That's all it said. Little did he know she was just a few miles away in Dunton Bassett, making wedding arrangements! To someone else.

It didn't make sense. Just a few days earlier they had been together. She would finish her jobs at the local farm and they would meet up to spend every minute possible with each other. That summer seven years ago John left school, so he was just biding time before starting college in September. He and Rose had become even closer.

He thought they had it all worked out. Inspired by stories told by her father about life travelling and building roads, it was then he made up his mind on a career in civil engineering. He had always liked constructing things and working out measurements and materials. Most of all, choosing the same line of work as Rose's dad made him feel closer to her and her family. It was one step further forward to joining the family firm. According to his logic anyway.

He listened for hours as her dad explained all the tricks of his trade – most you would be hard to find in any text book. But Rose's dad was sensible enough to advise John to learn his craft properly by gaining qualifications so he wouldn't be a glorified labourer all his life, as he was. That's what made John look for a surveyor's course. It led him to a college in Southampton.

He had a lift to Southampton with his Mum and Dad, who

dropped him off at the college before carrying on across to the Isle of Wight. His parents stayed over with his sister and then picked him up on the way back to Blaby. It was only when he arrived home and opened the front door that he saw Rose's note on the doormat. He recognised her writing.

She had written:

'My Dearest John
When you read this I will be miles away in Ireland. I don't know when I will be back. My auntie has been ill as you know and has now taken a turn for the worse. Mum and Gran decided it was best if we all went back.

Dad's still here but has been moved to a new site in Northampton, on a new motorway. We could not leave the children with him so we have all gone back.

But that's not all. Mum, dad, and Gran are pretty old-fashioned, as you know. It's not that they don't like you, but they think we're too young to be so serious. They said to tell you not to try to contact me. That we need to stop seeing each other. I feel it's for the best as well, especially as you will be going away to college. You need to concentrate on your studies, not me.

I will try to forget you but it will be hard. I know you won't find it difficult to meet someone else in Southampton. There are lots of other fish in the sea. Forget me. Most of all, forgive me.

All my love, Rose x'

His heart sank as he dropped the letter. Close to tears.

"Where are you going?" his Mum had asked as he rushed out to get his bike from the garage. He was totally bewildered after reading the letter.

"Rose has gone," was all he had said, striking out for the gypsy camp in the desperate hope that they had still not left for Ireland. But he was too late. He ran his fingers through the darkened embers of the camp fire. Cold. Rose had been gone some time. They would have travelled by train he guessed, to the nearest ferry port, and would probably *already* be in Ireland. Suddenly, his whole world was falling apart – empty.

For a while he had just stood there in the abandoned camp. Himself abandoned. Alone. Trying to imagine it as it had been just a few short days before. There were remnants of hay and straw left by the ponies. Discarded clothes pegs littered the ground where the washing line once was, and a bare patch on the grass verge showed where the vardo used to be.

But there was no evidence that Rose was once there, on that very spot. Just as he was about to get on his bike to ride off – to where? he thought - he remembered. They had a secret place where they left messages if ever John found Rose was not there when he turned up. It was a plastic box with a waterproof sealed lid. They could leave notes, or anything. On one occasion she left a ribbon skilfully woven in the shape of rose petals, surrounded by a heart. He still had it. The box was still there in the hedge to the side of the gate to the field. What was that inside? It wasn't paper. And it shone in the afternoon sun as he reached in to retrieve it. He prised open the lid to find a brass plate. It contained one word: "Jessie."

One heart-warming emotional surge flooded in to drown his despair. There was some hope. If only he could see her again. Was her letter a mistake? A lie? Would she still hold by her promise?

His perfect summer came to a tragic close right then.

CHAPTER FIVE

A Southampton winter – A St Ives summer

For a sixteen year old it was difficult striking out on your own. For John it was especially hard. He was losing his best friend (of over 10 years), the family home he had known all his life – with his parents – had disintegrated, and he was thrown into a new town at a new college not knowing a soul. Worst of all he had lost Rose – deepening his sense of isolation.

His first trip to Southampton a few weeks earlier *did* help. At least he had a place to stay and he settled into his hall of residence quite well. Fellow students were friendly enough – they overcame their own feelings of uncertainty at their new surroundings by being overly friendly – but he was just not interested in making friends. He found far greater solace in his own company, alone with his thoughts of Rose and all that had happened that summer. He was torturing himself.

The one thing that didn't suffer was his studies. He attacked them with an energy he found necessary to cope with the profound sadness. It was almost like a bereavement that simply would not leave him. He joined the college soccer team, discovering a new aggression that instilled in him a new enjoyment for the game. Perhaps the only joy he felt.

Half term left him with unwelcome gaps in his life – they seemed meaningless. At first he went over to stay with his sister Marie at her guest house on the Isle of Wight. His parents were always pleased to see him but he had to feign interest in anything they said to him. They noticed the change in him from the previous summer and all they could do was worry. But progress with his surveyor's course was solid and he was secure financially - and with a place to stay. So they were satisfied overall.

The first year at Southampton went very quickly, perhaps because his thoughts were always occupied by one thing or another – whether personal or academic. Now he was facing three months of...what? Then a solution appeared out of the blue.

His friend Ross, in Blaby, was leaving school that summer and had got a waiter's job at The St Ives Bay Hotel. It came with meals and a place to stay, paying the princely sum of £8.00 per week. John received a surprise phone call from him at the Spring Bank Holiday. They wanted a kitchen porter available to start in June. He applied and was delighted to get a return letter offering him the job - the first thing he had felt happy about for a long time.

During the Easter, May and Spring breaks he had helped out in the kitchens at his sister's, so she provided a reference. They had hoped he would work there the whole summer – especially his Mum and Dad – but they understood he wanted to spend the summer with his pal, Ross, instead. It was the best decision – actually the only decision – he had really taken since accepting his place at Southampton college. He was about to 'live' again.

As a seasonal worker he discovered it came with built in benefits: instant friends. Whilst he had a self-imposed self-isolation in Southampton, Ross wasn't about to let that happen in St Ives. Nor did he resist. It was a new routine he followed without complaint. It was a straightforward plan: Work hard – go to the beach at every occasion – go to the pub when not on the beach – look for girls. That was Ross' view on things anyway. John would have to 'jump back in the water' sometime, Ross said. If that *was* the case, then he had spent the whole winter 'dry'.

He had always called Ross a 'babe magnet', and not without a tinge of envy. Correction – not without a *lot* of envy. But it had always been the case so he accepted it. Before he met Rose he had begrudged it, but he accepted it. It was usually down to 'whoever Ross hooked up with had a nice friend'.

To be fair, John would never be one to sleep around or to take relationships *too* casually. The one legacy that Rose had left him – one that he valued above all else – was that friendship with a girl was pointless unless you connected at an emotional level. It wasn't that he feared he would feel guilty or unfaithful to Rose, but he was keeping faith with the kind of relationship they shared – even though no girl could come close to Rose. No matter how hard he tried to forget her.

So it was that he had a summer he could look back on with pleasant reminiscences over the coming winter months. Due to Ross' magnetism, he met and befriended several girls and enjoyed doing so. They were casual – some were only down on holiday for a week or two – but he didn't use them. He was able to fill at least one small part of the void left by Rose, the mere warmth in a girls' company. The fact that he knew - and they knew - their time together would be just a matter of days, often made it easier.

He found he could open up about Rose purely because of that. The backdrop of St Ives – with its soft sandy beeches, surf, clear waters and skies - provided the perfect setting. Somehow you felt you were under its spell, so distant in every way from 'normal' life.   In so doing, it drew out of you innermost feelings to a point where you felt so at ease sharing them. He was grateful to unburden himself in this way, even with girls he would know only fleetingly.

He was also pleased to see that Ross had stuck with the one girl towards the end of the season. So much so that he took her with him – or was it the other way round? – to Fuentaventura, in October. There was a mini-exodus of mainly surfers seeking a year-round sun that they hooked up with, saving sufficient funds to take them through to the following season in St Ives. At least that was the plan.

John was content to return to Southampton and his course, feeling partially healed, at least. He nursed one dream: to take Rose to St Ives, but that was never going to happen, he thought.

CHAPTER SIX

Another college year – another summer in St Ives

Returning to Southampton for Year Two of his course he stayed in their halls of residence again. Granted it was a fairly sterile environment, but that's what suited him. Keeping up the momentum in another academic year was his goal once more. With no distractions. It was fun in St Ives with Ross, but now it was back to business, or rather study. Feeling guilty at neglecting his family over the summer, he *did* pop across to the Isle of Wight at half term breaks, as well as the odd weekend.

He was puzzled by the fascination they had with the island but *they* seemed to love it, in contrast with life in Leicestershire. He called it 'Coventry-By-The-Sea'. After a few visits and not really relishing a whole summer there, he was resolved to return to the St Ives Bay for the following summer. He called the hotel at Christmas and they offered him a start the following June – with a pay increase to £8.50 a week. 'What's not to like?' He thought.

With end of term examinations over, he took the train down to St Ives. The journey took the best part of seven hours but he slept most of the way, arriving just after lunchtime after an early morning start. He couldn't have timed it better; he was greeted by blazing sunshine. The hotel was just a few yards opposite the station. Perfect. He checked into reception.

The chef was just finishing up after lunch so he came out to greet John for a brief chat in the lounge. Normally he wouldn't be allowed in the public areas of the hotel, but this was a one-off. This year it was a guy called Mike, from Plymouth replacing last year's chef, Manolo from Spain. He'd returned home. John was given the address of a council house just off The Stennack, where they put him up on a room only basis.

Mike asked him to report back at five o'clock for his evening meal, ready to start the shift an hour later.

Walking down the steps to the staff room at the rear of hotel he suddenly heard a familiar voice escaping from an open window. Or rather a familiar laugh. It was Maggie, his girlfriend up until he left St Ives the previous September. She gasped as he entered the staff room. "John! What are *you* doing here?" she said. "*This* is a surprise." She got up to hug him before sitting back down. "This is Pete, he works in the Still Room."

" 'allo mate. You the new 'potwash'?" There was no mistaking Pete's London accent.

"That's me, Pete. Can't keep away. Is chef serving our tea yet?"

"Should be," said Pete. "I'll come with you. Save our seats, Maggie." But they *were* the only ones there.

Mike was already in the kitchen preparing dinner for the guests, but first he had to cater for the staff. He filled their plates then they started back for the staff room. "Where are you staying?" John asked.

"I've got a place here, in the hotel" Pete said. "I started a month ago and got the last one available. You got a room up The Stennack?"

"Yes. Where I stayed last year."

"Is that how you know Maggie?" Pete asked.

"Yes. We went out together for a while." John thought that didn't go down too well with Pete, but said no more. It *did* register with him that Pete and Maggie would be sleeping under the same roof. He wasn't quite certain how he felt about that. Surely not jealousy? He and Maggie were seeing each other for only a few weeks just before the last season ended and he went back to Southampton. It was a funny relationship. They parted on good terms and never kept in touch over the winter.

But it was good to see her again. Pete and John sat back down at the seats Maggie had saved for them. He wasn't thinking too far ahead and how things might work between them this season. Right here, right now, as he looked across the table to Maggie his attraction to her was returning but he was uncomfortably conscious of how well she and Pete seemed to be getting on.

It looked like being another eventful summer...

Three months later John was turning the key in the lock to his door in the halls of residence. He was back in Southampton after another dream summer season in St Ives – until the dream turned to sorrow in the last two weeks. But he had to get over it, move on.

Now all he wanted to do was to forget the last weeks to focus on getting through his course with the same high marks as last year. He *had* to bury his memories of those final days and look to the future.

So that's exactly what he did, and he did so well that he was chosen for a prime placement for work experience, with a leading national civil engineering firm, on a key site in Plymouth. Further-more, he would be attached to them for his practical assessment in his final academic year, being transferred to Plymouth college.

June arrived and saw him on a train from Southampton to Plymouth station, from which he would take a taxi to a flat – found for him by the firm - on Mannamead Avenue. He was due to report to the site office of Peter Lundstrom by eight o'clock the following Monday. As he rode the first class carriage along the sea wall from Dawlish to Teignmouth he was reminded of why he just loved the West Country so much.

CHAPTER SEVEN

Work experience and a last term – now in Plymouth

His secondment to Peter Lundstrom was to start in June, so there would be no summer season in St Ives this year – nor the next. His attachment to the firm was a continuous stretch to August the *following* year. He would then have a month off before returning to college – this time Plymouth college – for his final academic year.

It was his first period of stability since he'd left his parents' home three years or so earlier. There were other students with their own rooms at the Mannamead Avenue ground floor flat – but on other courses and at other stages in their studies. There were some comings and goings during the twenty four months he was there., but he got used to it. Being at the far end of Mutley Plain it was on a main bus route for college, or an easy walk. Luckily, the firm loaned him a beat-up old Land Rover. That made him popular with his flat mates but he still kept his social life to a minimum.

The work experience took *some* getting used to, mainly the regular hours of 9 until 5, but it was varied work and a mixture of 'office' work in a Portacabin as well as being out and about.

However, once he *ha*d settled into a routine, he found he had spare time on his hands some evenings and at weekends. Occasionally, some of the guys in his flat would suggest they all go for a drink in Plymouth, rather than the students' union bar. It was a welcome change as the college concentrated on male-dominated professional subjects at that time. Although he was always searching for his perfect 'Rose substitute', that was looking remote.

One night they found themselves in Union Street and in a club called 'Tiffs In Town'. There were few alternatives in Plymouth at that time and he found the mix of discotheque and live bands a refreshing change. Then he noticed they were looking for bar staff, so he applied. If you counted private bookings they were open seven days a week, but he put himself down for Thursdays to Sundays for starters to make sure he could cope.

He could. And he did. And the extra money helped.

This was John's first glimpse of clubs seen 'from the other side'. He found it fascinating. The sad part was that some of those working as bouncers or bar staff were doing it 'to get away from the wife'. They used the job to meet other women. But he warmed to the sense of fun he had already witnessed in his seasons in St Ives. It was certainly there – and in spades.

After a while he got to know the regulars, which he loved because he was able to mix with people from different backgrounds, trades and professions. He felt more integrated into the city life, rather than remaining insular – which was the case of many of his fellow students.

To top it all, the DJ – Bobby – was brilliant and knew exactly how best to 'turn on' his audience. They loved him. The Sunday special was where they all lined up – sat down actually – on the dance floor in a long train, moving and swaying to the music in a set routine. Bobby had the whole place jumping to that. His other secret was on 'Superstition',by Stevie Wonder. Whereas other DJ's played it at the normal speed, Bobby twigged that it was too fast for most dancers to make sense of it. So he slowed it down a tad. It worked *so* much better. He was so popular, he was always being approached by other venues, like The Majestic, but he remained loyal to Tiffs, and the Tiffs' regulars remained loyal to him.

As a night club, there was nothing to rival it locally. On Thursday they even filled the floor with ballroom dancers of all things. That was an excellent change for those that worked there, with the clientele being more matures, it made a welcome change.

Best of all were the Christmas parties, the highlight of which was for The Ark Royal – for the crew of the Royal Navy aircraft carrier. The club was not small, but the amusing thing was that they needed *two* separate nights, so that *all* the crew had a chance to attend.

Of course, the master stroke was that the bouncers were

made up mainly of army and marine commandos, so there was never, ever, any trouble on the dance floor or at the bar. But *did* they drink!

The bouncers were a 'clan' all to themselves. If they weren't marines from the local military base, they would invariably be truck drivers. Either way they were big. And strong. Ironically, whenever a fight broke out – which was rare – they would deal with it without any fuss. Most often, nobody knew there had been any trouble. He never saw any of them throw a punch, not even in retaliation. Their method was simple: they would grab the unfortunate troublemaker in a bear hug – usually just one and unaided – carrying them out the front door into the street.

John once asked one of the bouncers how they did that, and why. The answer came back that they had such little respect for anyone not in the military, that they didn't regard them worthy of a punch! They were great guys to be on your side and John grew to really like and respect them – including the truck drivers.

Two things John noticed about himself when working in the club. Even though he was just a lowly barman, he didn't exploit any tips he was offered, and he never drank too much.

Another thing was that he resisted becoming predatory. There were scores of girls all out to enjoy themselves but he only took one girl seriously as a potential girlfriend. She was a regular on Fridays and Sundays. Week in week out he had girls galore passing before him but she was one of only a few who interested him. Strangely enough, girls seemed to find bar staff fair game and just as much a proposition to fellow club goers. He could never figure that out, but just went along with it. Why wouldn't he?

But this girl was different. She never had to approach them, they always found her. It was several weeks before he even spoke to her. He just watched when others 'tried to get to know her'. He had to laugh at himself. Whenever a guy seemed to be making progress with her, sat at a table with her, talking, making her laugh – I think the term they use is 'moving in' – he would get nervous, worried in case she left with him. Always she would blow them out before the end of the night. Always to his great relief.

Weeks went by and finally he got to talk to her. She usually came with three or four other girls but she outshone them all. It reminded him of how Ross was 'the babe magnet' when the two of them used to hang around together. She was the magnet in her group, but she seemed to like the other girls round her as some sort of protection. That said, once he did get to know her, enough to talk to her regularly on her nights at the club, he was surprised at how self-assured she was.

But it was often pure torture. He soon realised he was hooked just like the rest of the 'no hopers' – those he had watched try and fail so many times before him. The annoying thing was that she always smiled at him if he caught her eye, and was always engaging when they did have a chance to have a proper conversation. That was rare, however, and he could only snatch the odd fifteen minutes if he was on a break and she wasn't dancing.

Finally she agreed to see him outside of the club night, but not on a date. She would come round to his flat the following Sunday afternoon. It was all fixed by the end of a particularly heavy Friday night and he could hardly believe it.

His flat-mate Dixie answered the door when she arrived – right on time at two o'clock. Dixie showed her in and gave John a look of approval without her knowing, before he disappeared into his own room. He was just being curious.

"Lovely garden, John," she said.

"Seeing as it's warm and sunny, why don't we sit out there, then?" John led the way to the gazebo which was sheltered and still catching the afternoon sun. "I'm glad you could make it," he said.

"I have to be away by four," she said. "After all, I have to give myself enough time to look beautiful for tonight." She meant her usual night at Tiffs in Town.

"I couldn't imagine you looking anything else," he said. He meant it. He had only seen her in the half-light of the club up to now. In the full light of day she looked even more beautiful, even though she had dressed down to sweater and jeans. It was her piecing blue eyes, making her irresistible.

"How's the course going?" she asked. She knew he was a student.

"Pretty good, thanks. I'm actually on work experience at the moment, which is more interesting. It's mainly practical rather than study. We're at Marsh Mills, at the start of the new A38 dual carriageway."

They carried on chatting casually. She told him about her job as legal secretary for a local solicitors and her plans to get married in a couple of years when her boyfriend had a more permanent posting. That did rather put a damper on things.

"How long have you been going out with him?"

"Since school, actually. Four years now, "she said.

"You must trust him." It was more of a question. "Don't you worry with him being away at sea so much?" he asked.

"He trusts me, so why shouldn't I trust him?" She had a point.

"I'm glad you came, but why did you?" he said.

"I like you, John. I really do," she answered. "But I want us to be friends, even though I cannot go out with you. I know we have our moments at the club but I don't want you to read more into it. I don't think it's fair to you, which is why I agreed to meet you today, just to get things straight."

His heart sank. It sounded like an ultimatum. So final. "I wish we could be more. Believe it or not, I can't talk to other girls the way I can talk to you. But that doesn't mean I don't wish we could be more than friends."

"If anything changes, you'll be the first to know," she said. "I see something in you that I don't see in others, not even in my boyfriend, so I do hope we can still stay friends and do this again. As long as you understand it can't go any further. But who knows when I might need you." She caught hold of his hand, pressing it to her cheek. His heart leapt. There was only one other girl who had ever done that. "I'd better make a move," she said.

He offered to run her home, which she accepted. She still lived with her Mum in a terraced house in Stoke Village, a suburb just over two miles from him. She asked him to pull up before the junction with Albert Road, he guessed because she didn't want to be seen with him.

"We *will* do this again," she said. He swiftly moved round to the passenger side to open the door for her. She smiled. "Like you, I don't find many people I can talk to – not even the girls

– in the same way I can with you. It means a lot to me." With that she kissed him, surprisingly on the lips. "Bye, John."

"Bye, Rosemary," he answered. He stood there watching her as she turned the corner into Home Park. But she didn't look back. She didn't want to give herself away – for him to see the effect she was having on him.

"Almost perfect," he mused to himself. "Even down to the name, almost," he said out loud, as he began to drive slowly back.

CHAPTER EIGHT

Full time at Peter Lundstrom – Living in North Road West

As soon as he completed his final year at Plymouth college he had to give up his accommodation in Mannamead Avenue. It was for students only. He had to scour the local papers for lodgings which would take time so he took temporary accommodation. The chalet he found at Bovisand was in a superb location, but short-term. It was on a holiday park.

Then Ray and Bren stepped up. They were two pipe layers and about the same age as John so they got on really well. That was evident from the start.

They were the first friends he had really made at Peter Lundstrom who he would class as people he would socialise with outside of work. He had been on his work experience for a year before they arrived over from Ireland. He liked it because they were different again from his flat mates and students, who he found could be somewhat immature. His work-mates at the club were great to get on with too, but because they shared the same work pattern – and shifts – the opportunity to meet up outside of that was not all that easy. Ray and Bren turned out to be a breath of fresh air.

They were such good fun but it was more than that. He could sense they were genuine. They worked hard and they drank hard, but their generous Irish spirit came through regardless. He met them in The Patna on North Road West for a pint before going over to their lodgings, virtually opposite. They shared a room on a B&B basis, with lunch on weekends and laundry as needed.

It was how it was in those days. The landlady would fit as many single beds as she could into each room, with one wardrobe per bed. Ray and Bren had three beds in their room. Adding John as a third lodger was a formality especially as he came on their recommendation. Mrs Leek, the landlady, asked for two weeks rent in advance and it was a "done deal". He agreed to move in the following Sunday. Talk about landing on your feet.

As he drove back to his temporary billet at Bovisand that evening he reflected on how lucky he was. New job – that he loved; new digs – decent enough for now, and he got his washing done; and new friends. Although saving money wasn't really an issue they could even car share when it suited. John had his new Land Rover, courtesy of Peter Lundstrom, but of all the benefits this new arrangement presented, John valued the new friendships most. Last time he had student life to keep him socially busy; now there was a gap. Or there would have been were it not for Ray and Bren.

At Mrs Leek's B&B there were other boarders living away from home. Some worked on construction sites like themselves; others were on vocational courses retraining for a trade at the Adult Learning Centre in Plympton. It was for painters, plasterers, bricklayers, electricians, plumbers – that sort of thing.

There were eight boarders in all. Some of them went back to family at weekends. At each breakfast and dinnertime they would all eat round a large table in the downstairs room of the four storey Victorian terrace. It had probably been the servants' quarters back in the day, with the kitchen next door and scullery off that.

John thought the whole set-up was amazing in itself. The three of them worked together, ate together, socialised together, and slept together – that is to say in the same room. In singles. John was not actually their boss, so things worked out with no friction. But that was to change soon, slightly.

Every night they would go for a drink, usually in The Patna to begin with. At weekends that might stretch to The Archer, The Wyndham, each of them - like The Patna - named after the street they were on. They also stopped off at a new pub that had recently opened, The Valletort (after some medieval knight, they thought). It was on the way to Western Approach and the city centre. Sometimes The Newmarket might get a look in. The night it all changed was on one of their occasional visits to a small night club – more like a bar with music – above The Good Companions pub, popular with 'twenty-somethings'.

They arrived outside The Good Companions that Friday

evening by taxi. They knew that was ridiculous, which is why they did it. The joke was that The Newmarket, where they had come from, was a mere five minute walk away. If they *had* walked! They knew it was stupid but they still did it. The taxi drivers hated it in case they missed out on a higher fare, so they often told them it was stupid. They still took them as the tip was normally more than the fare. They did it to show off. And for a laugh. After all it reduced non-drinking time!

At nine o'clock, after a drink in the pub itself, they went upstairs. It was early for going to a night club but it had already been open an hour. Luckily there were three girls sat at a table. They were the only three people in the club apart from themselves and the staff.

It was one of those strange situations that sometimes occurs without any logic, reason, or planning. Had it been a packed club they would probably have just stood around the small dance floor drinking, weighing up girls without making any attempt to dance. Tonight was different. Getting to know these girls began easily – after all there was no competition on either side - and progressed so naturally that by nine thirty they had paired up. Bren was talking to Clare, Ray was dancing with Sue, and John was engrossed with Victoria. They were three student nurses. But not local.

Freedom Fields was a training hospital and, as luck would have it, the girls were new to the city and new to each other. They had only recently started training. They were attractive and surprisingly unattached. What boyfriends they had were either casual, or back home in Liskeard or Teignmouth.

As the night wore on the club *did* fill up. By that time it had become a fun evening and they all seemed to be pleased with how things had turned out. It was a great start to the weekend. The last dance came at midnight, slow of course, after which they agreed to see each other again. All six of them.

They offered to walk the girls back to Freedom Fields – where there were halls of residence – but the girls declined. This was probably because they had an early eight o'clock start – or maybe they did not want to raise the boys' expectations. Notwithstanding, that did not stop Victoria giving John a kiss on the cheek with "See you here on Sunday.

Eight o'clock." Sue and Clare had already walked on ahead, parting with just a wave to Ray and Bren.

If the night air was fresh – cold even – John didn't notice. He was wrapped in thought about the last three hours, reliving those parts where he felt he had especially connected with Victoria. "I think she likes you," said Ray, reading his thoughts. John merely grinned inwardly thinking, 'I do hope so'.

CHAPTER NINE

John and Victoria

Saturday came and, well, the pubs were open. Least-ways from eleven o'clock they were. Weekend pub sessions were a routine for Ray and Bren. John gave it a miss this time, making excuses about checking the traffic lights at the service road in Plympton. This meant Ray and Bren had to go on their rounds without him. But they were used to that.

He *did* check the lights on the site but it was secondary to his driving back into the city afterwards on a special errand. The six had arranged to meet outside the night club at eight o'clock on Sunday. John wanted it to be extra special. Since leaving college after his finals he still had no enthusiasm for a serious commitment to girls. He felt different about Victoria after just one meeting and didn't want to blow it.

'If the moment's right I will give her a little gift,' he thought. But what? He could over-do it and that might scare her. He didn't want to make the same mistake he had in St Ives, with Maggie. Plus, it might be too soon. He hardly knew Victoria. Even so, he felt compelled to go through with it. Dingles would be the ideal store. Or Debenhams. Within the hour he had found the perfect present. All he needed now was the perfect moment. But when might that be?

Saturday night came and, well, the pubs were open again. Mrs Leek always started tea early at the weekends. If any of her lodgers did work on Saturday it was usually only until lunchtime. John, Ray and Bren ate at five o'clock sharp and were safely in the pub by six. They chose The Pennycomequick, which would be on their way to Mutley Plain as they did the rounds.

John was a little apprehensive about going to Mutley. It was not too far from Greenbank where the girls had their lodgings. It was a natural alternative to the city pubs for them also. What if they bumped into them? What if they were with some other blokes? What if.....nothing like that happened? He was out-voted on all the counter-arguments he put forward, so off they went.

Nothing *did* happen to spoil the evening. It was just three lads out for a few beers. In those sessions they invariably talked about home. John missed out the painful bits about Rose on those occasions, but he did mention he had been friendly with Romanies originally from Ireland. Ray and Bren were familiar with how whole gypsy families had re-settled in England, dating back to the last century. They understood the closeness that bound those communities, largely for self preservation against hostile locals.

For their part, Ray and Bren explained how the general goings on where they lived, and safety in the area they had come from, was being severely affected by 'the troubles'. Day to day life was getting uncomfortable for everyone no matter which side of the divide you came from. Bren saw that Ray, his best friend and drinking buddy, was finding it increasingly difficult to keep out of trouble due to his volatile nature. Deciding to do something about it he persuaded Ray to take the boat with him across the water to seek work in England. He had a cousin already working on a site in Plymouth so they made their way south to see if they could get a 'start'. That was some six months earlier, since which time they had found Plymouth suited them down to the ground.

That Friday they performed to type by taking a taxi from their first pub, The Pennycomequick, to The Hyde Park at the far end of Mutley Plain. That represented quite a departure from the norm, namely, it was quite a long taxi ride. Usually it was a few hundred yards. This time they decided to 'work their way back home' in reverse as it were, *from* The Hyde Park taking in The Crown and The Fortesque before heading back to The Patna for a final pint. John left The Patna before closing time. He told them he needed an early night so he could finish off some plans for Monday, but he definitely didn't tell them about the present he had bought for Victoria. He definitely had to wrap it without them finding out!

Sunday came and the boys made sure they had clean shirts – and underwear (!) - for meeting the girls that evening. Mrs Leek threw in a laundry and ironing service into the rent. And

41

it *was* thrown in. It wasn't just about the odd socks but the fact that they might be someone *else's* socks. That often made them laugh. There were eight lodgers and four rooms so it was quite common for laundry to get mixed up. The permutations were endless.

Ray and Bren went for their normal Sunday lunchtime drink leaving John to catch up on some notes for his site meeting in Ashburton the following day. After lunch they chilled out - either in the dining room where the soccer was on the TV - or in their room. Tea was beckoning so they went upstairs to wash, after which they would get ready to go out.

John was dressed first and went down to ask Mrs Leek for a spare key in case they were late back. (Hoping?) 'Late' was any time after 11.30. "Are you two ready yet," he called up the stairs. He was impatient to get going.

Down the two flights his pals bounced never looking so clean. "Swift one first in The Valletort on the way?" Did he have a choice? He agreed as long as it was just the one. It was already past seven o'clock. He was getting nervous and needed a drink after all!

Shortly before eight o'clock John was waiting outside The Good Companions. His two pals were inside on the pretence of queuing for the bar in case it was busy. Soon Victoria and Susan arrived.

"Where's Clare?" he asked.

"She's got a bad stomach. She's sorry. Is Bren here? And Ray?"

"Yes. They're inside," he said. He was glad Sue answered. He would have hated it if it was left to Victoria to lie. That's if, in truth, Clare *didn't* have a stomach upset. "We'd better go inside to tell him." Instinctively Victoria took his arm, glancing upwards to catch his reaction at her immediate familiarity.

On hearing Clare couldn't make it Bren feigned disappointment. Not that he was bothered one way or another if he went out with Clare. He just didn't like to be left out, particularly as he and Ray were such good friends. "Still come with us," said Sue. But the shine had gone off the idea.

"Thanks, but I think I'll make my way across to The Wyndham. Some of the boys are going there to play pool. I'll be fine." He left.

"Shall we go up to the club?"

"I've got a better idea," said Victoria, "let's go to The Barbican. It's a lovely evening and we've been cooped up in the wards all day. Is that OK with you boys?"

"As long as there's a drink at the end of it," replied Ray. They set off, threading their way through the backstreets, some still cobbled, to the Mayflower Steps. On the way they noticed that a local artist, a famous international one, was painting a huge mural on the wall above his studio and shop. It was a collage of local characters – landlords, fishermen and boatmen, ladies of the night – and students. He even recognised one guy he had known the previous year, a Geographer he had befriended. He remembered the guy always did have a medieval look about him. He fitted in perfectly. John must have kept them all there ten minutes or so trying to spot people he did know. Ray soon lost interest, "Come on. The beer's getting warm."

They made their way past The Navy and on to the Steps where they read the plaque about the first settlers' crossing to America. "Let's try The Dolphin", said Ray, impatient as ever, but he took one look inside the door before turning, shaking his head. "Too many hippies. Let's go back to The Three Crowns."

This they did, finding a table to themselves by the window over-looking the quayside. "You're very quiet, John," Already Victoria was looking for a way into his thoughts.

"Yes. I was thinking how much I was missing ... the folks back home." He had nearly said 'Rose'. Victoria was only the second girl he had been able to connect with since she had left. Rose always had a way into his inner places just like Victoria seemed to be doing. Was it the image of Rose he had seen in Victoria that first time they met, just two days ago? A vulnerability? There was clearly a physical as well as emotional attraction from the outset. It was apparent just by the way they looked at each other, but with Rose there had been more. Something deeper. But it was still early days.

Sue and Ray were also ideally matched. Neither was afraid to drink just enough to remain coherent. They chatted non-stop, often punctuated by raucous outbursts of laughter as

Ray told one of his unbelievable tales. When challenged about its truth or if it seemed so far-fetched he had just one defence, "It's only a story!" He always got away with it. The one he had just been telling was how he challenged everyone to his favourite 'party trick'. He would take a wheelbarrow – empty, of course - and just by holding the handles at the very end, he would be able to lift the barrow fully horizontally in front of him. Although he was not tall, he was broad and stocky with tremendous arm strength. He never once failed to beat off all challenges. He often said he should take a wheelbarrow with him on one of their drinking sessions so he could play for pints.

Places where he could play for pints, however, were in pubs on the Barbican or just off the Hoe with an ancient cannonball behind the bar. Pretty much anyone could hold a ball easily in the palm of the hand, but the game was to hold it palm facing downwards. Ray would do this and ask to be timed; whoever held it out – straight out horizontally in front of them – for the longest, was the winner. He would always win, no matter how big the opposition.

Ray was sharing these stories of his prowess with his three companions, but then went back to talking to just Sue. But they were just a little noisy, which suited both their temperaments.

Victoria and John on the other hand spoke mainly in quiet tones. It was as if to emphasise that what one said was only meant for the other to hear. Generally it was small talk about everyday events and thoughts, but the more a personal disclosure became, it felt like a secret. Their secret. They opened up feelings they did not want to share with others. It was so similar to the first time he and Rose sat by the river, the day Jessie died.

"Gosh, it's nearly ten o'clock." Nearly an hour had gone by with himself and Victoria wrapped in their own world. "We have to be back in three quarters of an hour, otherwise they lock us out," said Sue, flashing Ray a cheeky grin. Again it was agreed that they walk the girls back to The Good Companions. From there they could make their separate ways to their lodgings. But they had to hurry.

Reaching Cornwall Street in good time meant they didn't

have to rush their last goodbyes. Sue was already 'devouring' Ray's face without any shame on her part or resistance from him. Victoria and John took it a lot slower. They agreed to call each other on Monday to arrange when to meet again. This time they wanted it to be just the two of them. As John and Victoria drew even closer, unaware of anything or anyone around them there was suddenly a "Take that, you bastard!" Feeling a sharp pain to his nose John was on the floor, blood pouring from his face. Victoria had been barged out of the way by whoever had landed the blow.

"Hey, what the f**ck are you doing?" It was Ray running over to wade into a hooded youth who had knocked his pal down.

He managed one solid punch before a Cortina drove up, door swinging open for the 'hoodie' to jump in. The car drove off with Ray in pursuit on foot, giving up after a few paces. "You OK, buddy?" he asked, as Victoria helped John to his feet. "Who the f**k was that?"

"Dunno, never saw him before. Never saw him *then*, either." He was dazed and in pain.

"It was my boyfriend...my EX-boyfriend," Victoria added quickly.

It looked worse than it was, with blood all over his clean shirt. John was holding his nose. "He came out of nowhere. From behind. Are you alright Victoria? Are you hurt?"

"I'm fine. He didn't touch me. He never has. Here, take this." He pressed her handkerchief to his nose.

Ray was looking around, just in case they decided to return. Hoping they would ."Sorry mate."

"Not your fault." said John.

It was Victoria who felt responsible. "He must have driven all the way up from Liskeard. I only spoke to him yesterday. On the phone, to break it off. He wasn't too pleased but I didn't think he would do this. They must have been driving around all evening, looking for me....for us. I told him there was someone else, I guess that only made it worse."

"You'd better come back with us," said Sue, "we are nurses, after all." She sneaked yet another cheeky grin at Ray as if to say it was in the plans all along. But they were hardly the lengths she would normally go to, just to get Ray – or anyone else - back to her room.

Victoria agreed, her handkerchief pressed on his nose to stem the flow of blood. They made their way to the girls' hall of residence, but not too slowly or they would miss the curfew.

"Wait here," they told the boys when they approached the gates at Freedom Fields, "we need to check it's all clear." Two minutes later they ushered the boys past the empty reception area and down the first floor corridor to where they had rooms, just two doors from each other.

"I'll give you a knock," said Ray, disappearing into Sue's room. John followed Victoria into hers.

"There's only the bed, I'm afraid," she said as he looked for a seat. She was closing the door quietly to avoid the attention of the night porter. "We'll have to talk in whispers, they check the corridors every hour. "Coffee?"

She switched the kettle on anyway. He eased himself back onto the pillow, surveying the room. The only clutter, if you could call it that, was the pile of study books and manuals on her desk. Just one chest of drawers and a wardrobe were enough for her clothes. Her neatly pressed uniform was hanging off the wardrobe door. Just two posters adorned the far wall – one of the human anatomy, the other of David Cassidy. Complete with sink and small fridge for essentials, the room was small but sufficient.

Waiting for the kettle to boil she found the aspirin. "Take these," she said, holding out a glass of water. By now the blood had stopped, as had the pain, apart from a dull throbbing around the bridge of the nose. "You'll have to make sure that sets straight."

"I guess if I'm going to get thumped at all I might as well get thumped by a nurse's boyfriend," he said.

"EX-boyfriend," she corrected him. "I'm *so* sorry. I had no idea. I just hope I'm worth it."

"I don't blame you, if I didn't know better I would say it was a plan hatched by Ray and Sue just to get us back here." He sat up, but still *on* the bed. "Thanks for the coffee." He sipped it slowly so as not to spill any on the bed cover.

"Can we just get *under* the top cover," she asked, "suddenly I feel chilled. It must be the shock."

"It was me that took the punch," he laughed, then lifted up the cover so that they could both get under. "Will you hold me, John?" He didn't need asking twice.

It was Ray's soft tap on the door to Victoria's room and whisper that awoke them. "Come on, John. It's quarter past two and the night porter's just done her rounds. We can slip out now." Only when he rose from the bed did he realise he had no clothes on. Neither had Victoria. Then it all came back to him. He kissed her as he eased himself to his feet. She was still asleep.

"OK, just let me find my jeans will you," John replied.

Victoria stirred and reached up, pulling him to her to kiss him good night, still only half asleep. "You'll have to get punched on the nose more often if that's what it does to you," she smiled.

With that she closed her eyes, drifting back into a deep restful sleep. It wasn't until the next morning that she discovered the gift he'd left. It was a silver locket with his picture in one side and a note, ' If you feel the same as I do, add your picture in the frame opposite. xxx' He had found his perfect moment.

Threading their way back along the corridor, past the reception where they came in, the boys quietly lifted the latch to the outside door and left.

Ray clearly had a similarly good time with Sue and was prodding John for details of his last three hours with her friend. John would have none of it. Victoria was the first girl he had slept with since Maggie, and before that, Rose. He was determined not to cheapen what had happened, fearing it might be shared with all and sundry in the tea hut on the construction site the following day. Besides, he didn't feel like it. His nose had begun to throb again and he needed painkillers. He had some in the glove compartment of his Land Rover back at the lodgings. It was the longest 15 minute walk he had experienced for some time...

CHAPTER TEN

John and Victoria

It was Bren who woke him the next morning at the usual time, just before seven o'clock. Ray was already up but in the bathroom. Neither of them could understand how he could consume so much beer the previous night but still be raring to get down for his bacon and eggs the following morning. John had just enough time to wash, dress, and have breakfast before they all piled into his car for the twenty minute journey to the site. Ray spent most of the journey describing in detail the night's excitement, his side of things that was, whether Bren wanted to hear it or not. He was five years older than Ray and starting to grow weary of adventures like that, especially the elaborate stories that always followed. John certainly didn't need reminding of the painful bits. He didn't add his side of things, merely grunting agreement when prompted.

The day went fairly quickly as they worked to meet deadline on the yardage to be completed that week. John was busy calculating the materials needed, making sure they were delivered. Just after five o'clock they were driving back to their B&B. Ray, thankfully, was fast asleep in the back after the first mile. He was exhausted – a combination of the day's toil and the previous night's exercise.

John was still nursing a sore nose but painkillers every few hours made it tolerable. He had decided on a quiet night in. Ray found a second wind after tea and managed to persuade Bren to go for a drink. Unusual for a weekday, they decided to go right into the city centre. Just for a change. That's when 'Round 2' kicked off. It was Bren now who was explaining to John what had happened that night. He took the opportunity to tell the story whilst Ray was downstairs watching the wrestling on TV. That was mainly to avoid interruption from an over-exuberant Ray.

"We started off in The Valletort, then for some reason Ray wanted to go to The Good Companions. I thought it was a bit strange. We normally went across to the The Newmarket next, before making our way further up town. It was almost as if Ray was expecting something to happen, looking for something and in a hurry not to miss it. We didn't have to wait long. His instincts were right. It was all over before I realised what was happening.

'Hey you, ya f**ker!' he called out, pointing to a Ford Cortina parked opposite The Good Companions. Before the guys in the car could do anything – there were two of them – he ran over to the open window on the driver's side, reached in and took out the ignition keys, throwing them across the road. 'Get the f**k out!' he shouted, hardly giving the driver a chance as he had already opened the car door and grabbed him by the neck. 'Stay inside!' he yelled at the passenger. He then began delivering the hapless driver several blows to the face. He went down immediately. 'Stay down, and stay away from my mate. Don't let me see you again.' he shouted. The last we saw was them driving off at some speed as we strolled into The Good Companions for a couple more pints.

It was packed for a Monday, but there was barely a sound as we walked up to the bar to order. After a minute or two they could see we meant no harm – no further harm at least – and the buzz of conversation started up again. Those looking out the window at the time swapped stories of what they had just seen happen outside. We never did pay for our drinks!"

With that John and Bren turned in and were asleep by the time Ray came up. He slept well that night too.

If John needed proof as to how the Irish stood by their friends that episode was enough. They became even closer friends, quite often going out as a foursome - Sue, Ray , Victoria and himself. And there was never a repeat of that night outside The Good Companions. Nor any night after.

Those were special times for John, and for Victoria he hoped, but sometimes other forces get in the way. It might have been John's ambition. Although he was qualified, he was still relatively inexperienced when it came to the new technologies and procedures that building Britain's emerging road network demanded. He was keen to improve and sometimes that can get in the way, overshadowing other priorities. Like relationships.

And relationships *were* blossoming. Victoria and John enjoyed themselves most when it was just the two of them, but as a foursome it *was* still a lot of fun. They would pile into John's Land Rover and escape from the city. He and Ray worked outside all the time of course, but for the girls it was always a welcome change from the confinement of hospital wards.

There were so many charming villages a short drive from the city that they were spoilt for choice. Many pubs were on the fringe of Dartmoor and offered a noticeably slower social pace compared with the city pubs. John found there was almost too much adrenaline in the latter. Ray thrived on that but, after days and weeks of that at work, John craved the more gentle pace of the countryside. He particularly enjoyed the peace that Dartmoor offered, when his thoughts often strayed to quiet times with Rose.

Ray was happy whatever the backdrop. He and Sue were good company. On their many excursions they would take in Horrabridge, Cornwood, Meavy, or even cross the border to The Spaniards' Inn just inside Cornwall. Often John and Victoria would pick out their best discoveries and return at a later date, just the two of them. They were special times.

Change is very often forced upon us and when it is we don't always welcome it. When that happens we have to make a decision. Whichever option we choose usually means a sacrifice. Or at least a compromise. Sometimes the casualty can be a relationship. John was arriving at one of those crossroads now.

The chance came for him to go on a specialist training course at head office. The upside was that it would keep him in the frame for future promotion; the downside was that it meant a solid three month stint away from Plymouth. Away from Victoria. They talked about it at length but inside John had almost made up his mind to take it.

Since he had met Victoria he was having the most fun he had enjoyed in years, so much so that those around him noticed how much it transformed his character. He was happier and it showed. That in itself made even the workplace a happier place.

Victoria was clearly good for him in so many ways. He should not take that for granted. Nor should she, as she clearly cherished their moments together. But could they withstand the pressures of being apart for long periods? They had each become so used to the other being around.

Her training was not without its challenges too. John helped her forget them completely as they both retreated into their own world – when Sue and Ray allowed them to.

D-Day – decision day – came, and they both agreed he should go for it. They would deal with the separation as best they could. But it would not be easy.

CHAPTER ELEVEN

John in London

It was *not* easy. The training really was intense. From the beginning and over the weeks that followed the geographical distance led to an emotional distance between them. His need for her was replaced by a need to succeed at the new challenges presented to him. He was barely able to think about anything else. It felt as though he was always playing catch-up. He had fallen short of getting on a university course because of his low entrance grades. That's why he had to settle for a more vocational approach to his chosen field. He welcomed that at the time. Now he was pushing himself to his intellectual limits again.

Victoria, too, found that the theoretical as well as practical side of nursing was going to be more demanding than she first thought. Unlike John, she found that when she could escape from day to day pressures she really needed him. She looked for him and he wasn't there. She called him at his London lodgings, left messages, received no call back. She became despondent, slowly giving up on him. With no word at all her imagination took over, laying unfounded suspicions before her.

Her weekend work shifts often got in the way. Compounding that, John found he was so tired after a full week of concentrated study that, by the weekend, all he wanted was sleep. A round trip to Plymouth was out of the question, even though he could sleep on the way. Phone calls became fewer and shorter. And for him there was one more problem. Something else easing itself in between them, ready to prise them apart.

He was still haunted by the events that had separated him from Rose six years ago now. He was yet to discover what those events really were so *his* imagination also took over. His mind invented so many reasons, all slightly different but all with the same ending. Despite his heavy training schedule he was left with at least *some* hours to himself – hours when he was capable of thinking of other things besides his work. As the weeks wore on he found those vacant hours increasingly filled by memories of Rose. Not only did they invade his waking hours, but also his sleep. Always the same dream.

In his dream Rose was there with him, but in the background there was always the threat that she would leave; that someone would take her away. She came to him; she went away; she came; she went. The dreams were so real that he almost felt her presence to an extent where he was holding her, where she was kissing him. Then she was gone. She was spirited away against her will but he could not make out the invisible force that was taking her. It was something *inside* her, something more important than him.

In his dream she was trying to explain, trying to tell him what it was. But he couldn't understand her, her words came out in a language he could not understand. After a while she would be climbing onto the back of the vardo with someone, a man he did not know or recognise. She was waving from the back of the departing vardo as that final picture gradually dissolved. She disappeared. She left him. Alone.

When he woke up, although the dream wasn't real the loneliness always hung around. Even the thought of Victoria was powerless to completely rid him of that terrible weight. The mood would last for days afterwards.

But his time with Victoria since the day they first met had been special. He didn't want to give up on her or on them. One day when he felt he was getting on top of his studies, and his emotions, he thought he would surprise her. He would hop on a train and just turn up. Out of the blue. In Plymouth.

By now she had moved out of the restrictions of the halls of residence. She, Clare and Sue found a ground floor flat just off Greenbank and moved in together. It was more expensive, but what price do you put on freedom? Unfortunately, that new found freedom led them prey to temptation.

When he boarded the Plymouth train at Paddington John was still tired, not having the luxury of a lie-in after a heavy week on the course. It was an early train and, being nearly a four hour journey, it would still be lunchtime before reaching his destination. Still, at least he could sleep on the train. He had voted against an overnight service fearing than the four changes and a journey time of over eleven hours would be more exhausting. The travel vouchers that his firm had provided enabled him to travel first class. That was a real privilege as it meant breakfast thrown in and comfortable seats. By Reading he was asleep, not waking until he heard the announcement for Exeter. So he missed breakfast.

At least he hadn't slept through the best part of the journey. It was just under an hour and a half to Plymouth. Leaving Exeter St David's station they were soon gliding along by the estuary and on to the coastline of Dawlish and Teignmouth, before forking off inland towards Plymouth. It reminded him why he was glad he had chosen the Westcountry after leaving Leicestershire and then Southampton. Travelling at seventy miles an hour just inches from the water's edge was a unique experience, and he almost forgot how hungry he was. He did manage a quick bacon roll and coffee on this final stretch of the journey and, as they left Ivybridge heading for his final stop he was at last feeling refreshed. He was actually looking forward to seeing Victoria again, hoping she would forgive him for turning up on her doorstep unannounced.

The one person he did tell was Ray. John bore a suspicion from what Ray was saying when he turned up to meet him off the train, that he and Sue had problems of their own. Whilst he was still seeing Sue – sort of – the fun side they had first shared 'when they were four', had dwindled. Sue and he did not see each other so often. She gave excuses that she had so much study to do. That she was either tired or that her shifts clashed when he wanted them to go out.

He knew where their new place was, so they took a cab from the station to where the girls lived. It was Saturday afternoon. They knocked on the door. It was Clare who answered. Her boyfriend stood behind her just inside the door.

He had been the real reason she had not turned up to the date with Bren on that second night. He and Clare had been going out together for two years, back home, but it was not until after Clare had started her training that they decided to get engaged. Soon after that he had moved to Plymouth to be with her. He actually found the flat first when he arrived as Clare was still in the halls of residence. He lived in the flat above the girls, sharing with two other lads. It was he who then told Clare about the flat below them when it became vacant.

"Victoria, Sue. It's for you," she called, not really speaking to either John nor Ray. Victoria came to the door first. A little tipsy.

"Oh," she said, "I wasn't expecting you." John sensed a shocked tone and awkwardness in her voice. It wasn't the welcome he was prepared for. "You'd better come in. I wish you'd let me know." He dropped his holdall in the hallway and followed.

Ray and John had already feared the worse. They entered what turned out to be the lounge. Three girls, three boys – now them. Who were the odd ones out? They noticed the open beer cans and a couple of bottles of wine being passed around thinking "Looks like a party. And we didn't get an invite!" he thought.

John's expectations were instantly deflated. The embarrassment they felt might have been easier to bare had it not been for the one who then proceeded to pick up a guitar – John's guitar - and begin to sing. It was clearly for Victoria's benefit, one of those soppy Bee Gees love songs. But what followed that was even more annoying - he played and sang it *so* well! Victoria was making him feel still worse by hanging onto his every word to the point of singing along with him. He felt like telling her that he had got the message but thought better of it. He didn't want to give her the satisfaction. After that, John always hated that song. And he definitely did not want his wretched guitar back. She could keep it.

Ray was amazingly calm. John half expected him to start throwing punches. He didn't. It was so unlike him. He didn't seem to care which of the three boys Sue was apparently "with". Instead, with a nod to each other in the direction of the door they left quietly. This was to the clear relief of Victoria and Sue which, in turn was a disappointment to John and Ray.

To be fair, the girls did have the courtesy to show them to

the door. John hardly spoke and couldn't remember afterwards what was said by the girls, other than recall a series of mumbles from Victoria interspersed with "sorry".

Sue was always the most outwardly demonstrative of the two, kissing Ray on the cheek followed by a prolonged hug. Victoria merely rested a hand on John's arm – instead of a handshake? - and hurried back inside where it had gone surprisingly quiet. Sue released Ray as he stepped into the street, moving across to put her arms around John, whispering "I'm sorry," as she pressed something – a note – into his hand before disappearing inside.

It was an awkward departure coupled with the realisation that whatever fire had been burning at the beginning, towards the end it had simply been extinguished by their own hand.

Because it was the end. And the flame had died.

But it was not the end of the friendship between John and Ray. If John was in any doubt of that, it was Ray's reaction when John told him about the note he had received from Sue. Once outside the flat and meandering through the back streets to North Hill, North Road East and then West to their lodgings, John pondered on the note. Should he tell Ray? "Of course," he answered himself.

"Raymond," he said, rarely using Ray's full name, I got this. A note from Sue as we left."

"What does it say? You haven't been carrying on with her behind my back, have you?" As soon as those words came out, Ray knew he didn't mean it, but he still had to reassure John. "I was joking. What does it say?"

"Just 'Call me next when you feel it's the right time,' followed by a number." John was as mystified as Ray at this.

Ray came out with the first theory, "Perhaps it's to explain what has been going on with Victoria. Sue and I were steadily drifting apart after you left, but I know Victoria was a bit messed up, just on what Sue used to come out with now and again." They left it at that, but it was further proof of the trust each had for the other. But to do away with any doubt, Ray reached across to shake John's hand as a gesture of friendship. They walked on in silence.

CHAPTER TWELVE

John back in Plymouth – his career progresses

John was due to return to the Plymouth site after his course in London and did so a few weeks later. He was looking forward to getting back even though he was impressed by the capital city and his home for three months. Not that he had many memories to fall back on, other than the daily grind of the course he had just completed. There were only five others being trained up, and they lived close to London so they went home at weekends. He never really made friends with any of them. Any spare time he did have was spent sightseeing – the usual landmarks and national heritage on everyone's list.

During any other spare time his thoughts drifted back to Victoria – until their break-up, of course. After that brief episode and sudden ending in Plymouth, it was Rose who now dominated his thoughts full-time. But he was still able to focus on his career, which his time away in London did allow him to do. In the few weeks after the break with Victoria he began to consider how to move forward on a new beginning. He needed a new stability in his life otherwise he would fail in everything he had ever dreamed of. It was another three hour plus trip during which he was able to mull over his new plan. He would get to work on it as soon as he got to Plymouth.

First, he decided to get his own place. He had been away for three months and had given up his bed at the B&B. It was for the best. He was on a steep career path which needed his full concentration. That meant early to bed on 'school nights' and cutting down on his beer consumption. He could manage both by having a place to call his own, albeit rented. If he could find a six month rolling tenure that would suit him best in case he was relocated at short notice, but he would have that stability. He had a week's holiday booked for his return to Plymouth. That would give him plenty of opportunity to find a new place, as well as to grab some quality time with Ray and Bren. By the following Friday he was moving into an end-terraced house all to himself in Lipsom Vale. He was due to start back at work on the Devon Expressway three days later.

He was looking forward to getting back into the daily routine of site surveying but he made himself one promise. He would dedicate himself to getting on faster in his career – looking out for more new opportunities to get ahead and make something of his life. And that's what happened, but not exactly as he expected. Things were moving fast in his chosen industry. Vast sums were being spent on moving Britain ahead, encouraging inward investment with substantial subsidies to foreign companies in key manufacturing. That required a better infrastructure and road network. He was becoming well-equipped for that 'bigger picture' but surprised that his next 'project' was to take on a much smaller, community-based objective. As it happened he was pleased to be offered this second opportunity to help him over his split with Victoria. As he was about to be told, it would look good on his CV.

He had come out of the three month course with a further certificate to add to his surveyor's charter. On his first day back at the Plymouth site he was called into the site engineer's Portacabin. His boss, the Chief Engineer, was interested on how well the course had gone, congratulating John on his certificate. Then he got to the main reason he had called him in.

"I want you to go up to Teignmouth for a month or so," he said. They're doing a feasibility study for a bypass avoiding the town. They need our help. If you're up for it we can second you to the Project Leader – a town councillor – for as long as it takes. It will be for several weeks at least, maybe even months. They haven't got your level of up-to-date technical expertise and it's not worth them employing someone for such a short stint. It will be a kind of consultancy position but you'd still be on our payroll. It'll look good on your CV because you'll have to consider the bigger picture – environmental issues, traffic flow, relocation of key services like schools. You'll have to make formal presentations to committees, so brush up on your diplomacy. Interested?"

John didn't have to think about it. It was just what he

needed – if only to take his mind off other things. "What about accommodation? I've just taken a flat in Lipsom Vale."

"Hang on to it. Where you're going is likely to be early mornings and late evenings, with some weekends," the Chief Engineer said. "It's best if we put you up in Teignmouth during the week. There's The Royal Hotel on the sea front we can get on a long-term rate. You'll be quite comfortable there. Of course, you can still pop back to Plymouth when you do have free time."

John thought that was the best of both worlds. He could always come back for the odd day or two if he missed his pals. Ironically, when the new motorway was built between Plymouth and Exeter the drive time to Teignmouth would be halved. But that was still a couple of years away.

With most of the important aspects covered and agreed John went home to pack. He told Ray and Bren about it then drove to Teignmouth that afternoon to check into The Royal Hotel. He was due in the council offices in Bitton Park the following morning at nine o'clock for his initial briefing.

From a surveyor's viewpoint it was fairly straightforward. There was more than one option for the route the bypass could take, each with its own benefits and pitfalls. Relocation of certain key buildings – like to local school – was one hot issue with the town's traditionalists. He was warned that he might meet with some resistance from locals whichever option he favoured. Some of the most characterful and historic areas, with period cottages and shops run by family businesses for decades, might have to be acquired by compulsory purchase. Those costs had to be factored in and such negotiations represented a new dimension for him. Then there was the disruption to the community to be considered. How do you put a price on that? His boss was right. Diplomacy was something he would have to develop, even at his young age. He would be the youngest on the team. Maybe he *should* grow a beard.

After his briefing and scrutinising a map of the town to identify key features, landmarks and pinch points, it was suggested he take the rest of the day off to walk the town to take in the general atmosphere and layout. This would take him up to five o'clock at least. He didn't have to report back to Bitton Park until the next morning where he would be shown his office.

During his teenage years in Blaby he had been an avid fan of the live concerts at The De Montfort Hall in Leicester. From American artists like Dion, Del Shannon, Chris Montez through to The Rolling Stones, The Searchers, The Hollies and – to cap it all – The Beatles, he had seen them all. Too many to mention.

He had see The Beatles twice. The second time the screaming girls spoilt it. He couldn't hear a thing – plus he had to stand throughout the whole concert, even though Melv and he had seats. As soon as the band appeared on stage, the girls in the audience stood up to scream. Then, because they couldn't see any better than if they had remained seated, they decided to stand on the seats!

Not long before he made the south west his new home, The Beatles had embarked on their 'Magical Mystery Tour' of the Westcountry. They had bought a touring coach and dressed it up in psychedelia before filling it with bit-part actors and 'ordinary folk', with the aim of filming their exploits. Of course there was music throughout and the usual messing about – or rock groups' typical attempts at slapstick humour.

Teignmouth was The Beatles' first night's stopover – at The Royal Hotel. John had a suite pre-booked by his company, but he could hardly believe his luck when the girl in reception announced he was booked into the same room George Harrison had stayed in! Laying his head on the pillow on that first night he thought, 'Wow. I'm sleeping in the same bed George Harrison shared with Patti Boyd.'

That was the last thing he could remember before waking up to the alarm the next morning, for his first full day of his new project.

His boss at Peter Lundstrom was right when he said he would be working full-on to meet the deadlines. Whichever direction the bypass was to take, the impact on the town would be significant. The pro-bypass lobby had strong opposition from those wanting to preserve its heritage. As a result there was a series of consultations and open meetings before a public enquiry was conducted and, hopefully, a plan to satisfy all parties could be agreed. Near enough at least.

He had become used to finishing before six o'clock then returning to The Royal Hotel for dinner after which he was ready for bed, even if that was just to watch the TV in his room. It was Friday evening before he remembered the note Sue had passed to him several weeks before. After dinner he decided to call.

CHAPTER THIRTEEN

John and Sue get together

"Hello, is that Sue?" The voice at the other end of the phone was female, but didn't sound like Sue.

"It's her mother. Who is this?"

"Oh," he paused, "I'm a friend. John. From Plymouth."

"Well she's actually in Plymouth now. You've reached her mother. This is a Teignmouth number. She'll be back home tomorrow. Do you want to phone back then? She should be in about mid-day. By train."

"OK. I will. Thank you. I'm also in Teignmouth myself, now." With that John replaced the receiver. "Unbelievable," he thought, "She's coming here tomorrow. How weird is that?"

He wasn't sure whether Sue's mother would tell her beforehand that he was in Teignmouth. Just as well because he wasn't certain he would be in town himself tomorrow. With the weekend free he was half thinking about catching up with his pals back in Plymouth. Then he came up with a plan. He would surprise Sue at Teignmouth station the next day.

Saturday came and he decided to miss breakfast. He deserved a lie in. Goodness knows he needed it. His plan was to wait for the 11.45 from Plymouth. He could have a coffee in the station cafe before the train arrived and see if she got off. Then he would jump out to surprise her as she was walking through to the car park.

His heart raced as the train was announced. He hadn't expected to be so excited as he got up from his table to take up position where arriving passengers would exit. "Had she made the train?" he was talking to himself now. The mainline service from Plymouth changed at Newton Abbot where she had to take a local commuter to Teignmouth. Otherwise she would shoot past straight to Exeter without stopping if she stayed on the Penzance to Paddington train. Ten minutes late the three carriage local commuter pulled into Platform 1. Yes. There she was.

She only had a hold-all so she was walking quickly. He

noticed how her abundant auburn hair cascaded over her shoulders as she hurried along the platform. He laughed when he thought how appropriate her platform shoes were in this context. She was quite a classy dresser and decided she wanted just a little extra height today. But why?

"Why do people always hurry when they get off the train?" he asked himself. He understood why if they had an appointment to go to, were late for work, or if they were meeting someone and the train was late. It *was* late. By ten minutes. "Surely she's not meeting someone.?" He felt a slight panic. "There's only one way to find out."

"Ta-daaaa!" he was laughing as he pounced out in front of her.

"Ha! There you are," she grinned, as she jumped back feigning surprise. "Sorry I'm a bit late." She dropped her holdall, raising herself on tip-toe to kiss his cheek. She laughed to herself, recalling why she knew she would need her platforms.

"How did you know?"

"Mum told me, she told me that you'd phoned and were in Teignmouth. Then I thought, 'I bet I know what he's going to get up to'. And I was right!"

"Where to, m'lady?" he asked as *she* took hold of *his* arm.

"First I have to drop this off at Mum's," she meant her bag, "then I'm all yours." The way she looked at him with that last remark triggered a long-forgotten feeling in the pit of his stomach. He knew what she meant, but with Sue that could be taken either way. For the first time he realised how attracted he was to her.

They soon had the day to themselves. Her Mum lived a few yards away in Bickford Lane. John knew where he was because this was one of the possible locations to be affected by the new bypass. Sue introduced him to her Mum, Joyce, but quickly made her excuses to go out straight away. She was dying for a catch-up with him, not only after the sad break-up several weeks earlier, but it was well over three months – before his training course – since they had a proper chat. She was still with Ray then and he was with Victoria.

"Come on then. Spill the beans," she coaxed. "What are you

doing *here*? Have you moved for good?"

He took her through his spell in London, his brief return to Plymouth, and how he had ended up in Teignmouth. He missed out the bit about it being on a temporary basis, but told her he rented a place of his own in Plymouth.

"That's OK then," she said after he had brought her up to date. "I can have you in Teignmouth or in Plymouth. It's 'Win,win.'" Then added, "What's so funny?", as he burst out laughing at the way she put things. But that was Sue. She just couldn't help herself. Half the time she didn't realise what she'd just said.

"It depends what you mean by 'have'," but by now she was laughing too at the thought. They walked into town and along the promenade, 'just like a courting couple', John was thinking. By now he was starving. "Shall we have a bite to eat?" he suggested.

The place they agreed on was The London Hotel. It had a full menu in the evening but lunchtimes the speciality was The Carvery. Plus it had a relaxed bar-style which suited them both. The restaurant was always busy, making it even more perfect. They could talk without being overheard. They were both already having such a good time. It *was* like being a courting couple - on a first date.

Sue wanted to talk as much about *her* break up with Ray as about *his* with Victoria. When he was with Victoria he would often catch Sue watching him out of the corner of her eye. He suspected she was even eves-dropping on their conversations whilst apparently talking – or trying to talk – to Ray. Leading up to the time when they did break up, John felt that Sue and Ray's relationship was heading for an inevitable conclusion anyway.

John used to stay over with Victoria whenever he could. That was when she lived in the halls of residence at Greenbank, and as long as he left by 4 a.m.. Making love for them was one way they developed their spiritual connection. It reinforced all the feelings that they shared most. Perhaps because of that – when they took out the physical togetherness and were forced to live so far apart – that was when they learned to exist without *both* sides to they relationship.

Sue arrived from a different direction when it came to herself. Making love for her up to that point had been mainly a physical attraction. She never let on but she had long wanted to explore a more emotional side – and with John. She envied the closeness she witnessed in him and Victoria. Perhaps he had always sensed it in her too, but ignored it, being totally immersed in Victoria. The way things had started off between John and Sue it looked like that was going to change, and very soon.

John rarely drank during the day, even when he lived with Ray and Bren. Today he made an exception, his carvery supplemented by two excellent pints of Courage Best Bitter. His favourite. Sue preferred white wine, responding with two large ones. They poured out their feelings about everything, to their mutual relief. It was what they needed, almost like a therapy. With the pressures of his new project out of mind - at least until Monday - he was at last able to relax. He was grateful to Sue for that. She was so easy to get on with; he could forget about everything else and be himself when he was with her. He could behave naturally and without pretence. Sue found that she could be equally relaxed with John. Most of all she needed to share how things had been with Ray after John first left. Right then, Sue and John were good for each other.

Sue was strikingly attractive – not only for her flashing green eyes and her amazing shock of hair, but for her outgoing personality. At first some would say she was flirtatious, but it was more than that. She was generous and genuinely interested in people. When she wanted to be! People warmed to her. When she directed all this towards just one person, in this case John, she was impossible to resist. John wasn't about to, as he stole a kiss from her without warning.

With lunch taken care of and drinks finished Sue made the next move. "I've never been *inside* The Royal. Do you want to show me round?" How *could* he resist? Cutting through the back streets once more they soon arrived at Den Crescent and The Royal. Not bothering about the lift they took the stairs to the first floor. John's room was just a few yards down the corridor. So much for his showing Sue *around* the hotel. He fumbled for his key, unlocking the door, they went inside. It was a` luxury suite!

The view from the front balcony was stunning, looking out to sea. Sue hardly noticed. Unable to help himself he moved forward, kissing her face and neck as they stumbled towards the large double bed. It was enough just to be holding someone, with someone who mattered and who understood you - as they now understood each other. It was not long before they undressed each other, spreading the covers over themselves before fulfilling the need they had felt for so long, but without really knowing.

When he awoke it was dark. John switched on his bedside lamp. He looked over at Sue. "I've been watching you for ages," she said. She had, long before *he* stirred. "I've often dreamt about this moment. I couldn't say anything when you were with Victoria. Besides it wouldn't have been fair to Ray, seeing as you were best friends. But you can't deny your own feelings forever. I couldn't."

"You've always been special to me, Sue," he said, "even though I couldn't say so either. You've got something Victoria doesn't have, couldn't have. You're such a lovely person and show an inner happiness. But it's more than that. You want those around you to be happy. Those who matter to you. Funnily enough, that's one part of you that you share with Ray. I don't need to tell you how caring he is, underneath all that toughness, even if he might knock seven bells out of someone he doesn't like."

"Perhaps that's what I love about you, too," she said. "I must admit I was a bit jealous of Victoria. Were you envious of Ray?"

"That is so unfair," he laughed. "But it made me think, 'Why can't we love another person, without it being a betrayal?' I don't mean in a physical way, though. That *would* be weird." Suddenly he thought of Rose. Would his dream of meeting her again ever go away?

"I see. Maybe if you love the second person in a different way from how you love the first, that's alright?" she offered.

"But you'd better not try that one with me!" They both laughed, but realised what they had just said to each other.

"So you're saying I love you, are you?" he asked. For the first time ever he thought he saw her blush. The bell for dinner sounded, saving her from having to admit what she already knew. "Are you hungry?" She was starving. It had been over six hours since they had eaten.

John went down to the restaurant ahead of Sue to ask the head waiter to set his table for two. Sue joined him a few minutes later having phoned her Mum from the lobby to say where she was. They ordered their food but this time chose soft drinks rather than beer and wine. "Teetotal are we now, John? Afraid where it might lead?" she teased.

"You can always stay the night." He was testing her.

"Whilst I'd love to...." she paused, "I should really spend *some* time with my Mum." John's own sense of disappointment surprised him. But he agreed it was for the best. They finished their dinner, but slowly, savouring the time they still had together before he would walk her home. Making it last.

They agreed to meet on Sunday morning. Sue would come to The Royal for breakfast. They served until ten thirty so they could both have a lie-in. Albeit separately. Then the day would be theirs again. Sue's train back to Plymouth wasn't until just before seven o'clock that evening.

It had been a perfect day. A perfect first date you might say. They appeared to be of the same mind when they paused to face each other, in Lower Brook Street, just so they could take the longest time to say goodbye, capturing all the passion of that afternoon. Finally she released her hold and took the few last steps on her own to her Mum's, turning briefly to smile as she rounded the corner into Bickford Lane.

Sunday morning could not come soon enough. John had slept so well, barely stirring. He was washed and dressed by nine thirty and decided to call Ray. Mrs Leek would have finished breakfast by ten o'clock. That would be just time enough for John to tell Ray about Sue, before she arrived for their breakfast at The Royal. He went into the lobby to make the call.

"Is that you, John?" it was Ray, he had been called to the phone from the dining room where he was just finishing his third cup of tea. Drinking the night before always made him thirsty.

"Yes. How are you?" John had half hoped Ray had gone out to fetch his Sunday paper so he didn't have to say what he was about to. After a short wait he had even thought about replacing the receiver... but he held his nerve. " I have something to tell you."

"If you're pregnant, then I'll deny it!" Ray rarely told jokes, none that were any good anyway. "Seriously. Are you alright? You sound a bit strange."

"Well, you remember that note Sue passed me? The day we all split up?"

"Yes."

"It's just that...well....we're seeing each other. She's with me now. In Teignmouth. Her Mum lives here."

"Is it my permission you want?" He pretended to be annoyed.

" Yes...I mean no... I - "

"I'm happy for you, John. Really. For you both," he put his friend at ease. "You're my mate. Always will be. And if she's going to be with someone else, I'm glad it's you. You deserve each other. 'You have my blessing, my son.'" he said, mocking his own church. "Take care, mate. Take better care of Sue."

John stood in the lobby of The Royal in sheer relief. He heard the receiver replaced at the other end. "Who was that you were talking to?" It was Sue. How long had she been standing there?

"I called Ray."

"Why? To compare notes?" She wasn't joking.

John felt a disappointment at being challenged, but kept his cool. "No. Not at all. I just had to tell him. To be out in the open about us. I've had enough secrets and deception in life so far. It never ends well. I felt he should know. It's a simple as that."

"Sorry, I really shouldn't have doubted you. I'm so sorry. Forgive me." She circled her arms around his waist to draw him closer.

"You're forgiven," he said with a kiss, pulling back too slowly as she released him to aim a smack at his shoulder.

Playfully. They went in for breakfast.

Sue was especially interested in John's project. It was *her* town after all. The primary school she had gone to was at risk of being bulldozed. He had to be quite careful what he said for fear of upsetting her. Not only that, all discussions prior to the public hearing had to be kept under wraps and nothing leaked beforehand. John felt uneasy about the political aspect of his new job, as well as a sense of guilt at hiding things from Sue. It was all new experience for him.

"Shall we take the ferry to Shaldon?" It was Sue's idea. John thought you could only take the bridge across but The Royal Hotel was literally minutes away from the ferry landing. They cut through to The Strand before turning into Lifeboat Lane and Back Beach. After a short wait for it to motor in from Shaldon, and letting the other passengers off, they were soon on board and on their way to Shaldon Beach. "As kids, we used to swim across to that island in the middle, over there towards the bridge," she said. It was quite safe as long as we waited for the tide. It's called The Salty. See – there's even grass growing on it. It's like a real Treasure Island."

It had been windy on the boat, blowing Sue's long hair across her face which she continually had to sweep back. John sat behind her as they faced the bow. He loved the smoothness of her face and how it was lightly freckled, common in some girls with such strikingly auburn hair and soft complexion. They would have called her a redhead in America he thought with some amusement. "What?" She had turned quickly and caught him watching her.

"Nothing. Just discovering how beautiful you are. Rediscovering"

"Rediscovering? I thought it was obvious the first time." But she couldn't help feeling comforted, reassured that he found her so attractive.

It was John's first visit across the river to Shaldon. He marvelled at how quaint it was in contrast to Teignmouth. The distinction between one - a village, and the other - a town, was striking. "Come on, let's go up to the botanical gardens."

Signposted from the main street it was gained by a steep

gradient off Horse Lane from Marine Parade. The climb was well worth the effort. They peaked through the trees and over the bay towards Exmouth. But just below them he found the view across the mouth of the estuary and Back Beach, overlooking Teignmouth, was equally picture postcard.

Sue explained how they would sometimes come to the botanical gardens from school for nature lessons in the small lodge in the middle. John wished he had his camera but planned to return armed later in the week. It would provide a panoramic sweep of the town, including the approach road from Salcombe Dip, through the centre of town, on to the Dawlish Road and then up past Eastcliff car park. It would be the perfect backdrop for his project presentation.

The lawn was dry – dry enough for them to lay down, side by side, facing up to the cloudless sky, without a blanket. It reminded him how he and Rose had laid just like this in open fields in his own village, so many times before. But Sue was all the comfort he needed right now. And she was real.

They remained there almost motionless and virtually without speaking for an hour. It was enough that they had each other. That was all they needed. They took a slow tour of the gardens before they made their way back to the ferry.

He marvelled at how close they had become in just two short days. Her glance back at him as they climbed the ramp onto the return ferry told him she felt the same, how she was checking to make sure it really was not a dream and that they were indeed together.

Six o'clock came all too soon. It was fortunate that Sue's Mum lived literally down the street to the station. It meant they still had plenty of time before they had to make the train just before seven.

"I hope the train's late," she said as they stood on the platform She pulled him towards her. "I don't want the day to end."

"It *will* never end, if you never forget." He knew from experience.

CHAPTER FOURTEEN

A spell in Teignmouth – his love for Sue

John's secondment to Teignmouth Town Council lasted for three months. When he first took up the post, whilst he did not relish the thought of having to negotiate the compulsory purchase elements of the project, it would look good on his CV. Towns-peoples' lives and even livelihoods would be affected by the bypass. Some would benefit but there are always losers. That part did not sit well with him. He had put forward two alternative proposals, balancing all the factors but prioritising the community impact as a leading issue over-riding all others. It was then up to the people to accept the one favoured by the council in a referendum. John was heavily involved in the committees leading up to that point, but he was glad he did not have to cast a final vote. He found it hard to be impartial.

One option did worry him and occupied a lot of his attention. It was the threat to the primary school with demolition and relocation. It was as if they were wiping out history. But he was relieved that even if that route was selected, he had managed to 'save' Sue's Mum's house. He had become fond of that part of town. The old part. He came to know and love the local families who lived there, many of whom went back generations.

A few doors up from Sue's Mum's was a Mrs Osborne. She was typical of those who made up the true fabric of the community. Her husband had suffered in previous world wars to return 'damaged'. But she managed to make ends meet by taking cleaning jobs to support her husband's income, and after his injuries rendered him unable to work.

She even had a son-in-law who had served in Bomber Command and was shot down over enemy territory. Missing In Action for several months, luckily he had come back - from a POW camp - at the end of the war. But changed. Quieter. More responsible. Once a rebellious youth, his strong sense of duty took over as he knew what he had to do when duty called. Always a brave lad, he had volunteered for the RAF a few months before he was strictly old enough. He survived several sorties unscathed, before finally being shot down over enemy occupied territory. He parachuted from his burning Lancaster, his boots being blown off his feet as he jumped. With the aircraft being hit badly, he didn't have time to tighten his bootlaces first.

Eventually he was among those liberated by Patton at the end of the war. Fearing him killed, his father had suffered badly, mentally. He thought he had lost his son – his second son so his butchers business suffered. When his son did finally return home safe to a surprised – but delighted – family, faithful to tradition his son stepped into his father's shoes. He ended up working the family butchers business until he retired.

These were just some of the stories that Sue's Mum told John, making her proud to be part of such a tight community. It was that quality he was determined to preserve. He had discovered the 'soul' of the town, and he wasn't about to let it die.

Sue's Mum was a good friend of Mrs Osborne. She was especially fond of her granddaughter Jane, who would often call round after school and at weekends. Jane was always willing to help, whether it was to take Joyce's milk in out of the hot sun, or nip to the shops for her. It was a solid neighbourhood which John was pleased to protect from so-called progress. His instinct told him the lessons learnt - like those learnt by Jane at the knee of people like Mrs Osborne - would ensure that the best community values would live on in Teignmouth. For those reasons he felt that the bricks and mortar that made up such communities were worth preserving.

Sue and her Mum were of similar type. Her Mum worked in the local family store – Hitchins - and had raised Sue on her own for the last ten years. Sue's father was killed in a fishing accident and left no pension. John considered it commendable that Sue's ambition was to return to Teignmouth after her training to work in the Community Hospital. That ambition might be challenged if she became too used to the heady city life of Plymouth. John thought that was unlikely. He never failed to be impressed by how grounded

Sue was despite her fun-loving side. She was more likely to be coaxed away by a career-driven professional man and then be relocated somewhere else. Whoever might that be...?

Even that was not such a fanciful idea as the weeks wore on, and the more she and John enjoyed each other's company. They did take every opportunity to see one another, as long as Sue could avoid weekend shifts. Partly to keep Sue's Mum happy they alternated their weekends together between Teignmouth and Plymouth. But news of her Mum becoming ill with cancer changed all that. As her mum got worse Sue took the decision to suspend her training, devoting what nursing skills she had to be her mum's full time carer.

Like a lot of crises some of their effects extend way beyond the immediate problems associated with them, or those immediately involved or affected. Sue's commitment to her Mum was total. She had witnessed at first hand the hard life she had endured in the years after her dad had been killed. Ignoring her Mum's protests she decided to dedicate her full attention to making her Mum as comfortable as possible. But that meant compromises. Unfortunately this level of dedication left little time for her and John. He was now back in Plymouth full time. Even a few hours together in the evening were now out of the question.

Longer periods at weekends were equally rare. They sensed a deja vu as they started to drift apart almost without realising. Could it be a 'John-and-Victoria' situation all over again? One significant change was the effect all this had on Sue's general demeanour. The burden she had accepted was wearing her down, but she did not see it as a burden. This was her Mum, who she loved. She didn't want anyone else to do it. But she was becoming depressed to the point of not being able to enjoy what little time she and John did have together. Sue's Mum was terminally ill and their plight was also desperate. John was saddened when he finally had to come to terms with the change in Sue and admit that they had a real problem.

He was powerless against the change. He was totally sympathetic to what Sue was going through virtually single-handed. Sue, for her part, could also see the affect she was having on John's happiness. When she called him to end their relationship he was hardly surprised but it didn't make it any easier. Their final words to each other were hard: that they still loved each other no matter what.

The Devon Expressway site had now moved further north towards Exeter, but only as far as Ivybridge and Lee Mill. Ray and Bren usually travelled to the site separately from John. One reason for separate journeys was that the contractor had to make up for time lost through bad weather, so pipe-layers like Ray and Bren, kerb-layers and fencers, were all on over-time. But not John.

Even so, they managed some drinking sessions together. John was grateful for the continued friendship. His job kept him fully occupied during the day but he needed their companionship in the evenings. Some evenings. He never could match them pint for pint. During the time he was away in Teignmouth the Ray-Bren Irish contingent had grown. In traditional fashion the prospect of good money earned on a new, urgent road construction had attracted more labour imported from across the Irish Sea. Much-needed labour. That meant much-needed brothers and cousins...

In the usual traditional fashion, the 'personal recommendation' of friends and family led to Ray's older and younger brother joining the fold, plus two cousins. This unfortunately did not moderate the consumption of alcohol. Beer volumes increased on these evenings – especially weekends – because there were now seven thirsts to quench. Once upon a time there were only three. Mrs Leek was never short of lodgers. Taxi drivers were never short of short-journey fares, but now they needed two cars per trip!

This is where his recent experience in Teignmouth helped. His role as surveyor developed from the mere mechanics of converting plans to the finished article to reading people and finding out what made them tick. In the case of Ray and his extended family it meant that John could apply his newly found skills in two ways: first, he could see when a quiet drink with the lads was going to develop into a session; second, he could anticipate when a session was about to deteriorate into an argument, or even a fight. This new 'early warning system' of his enabled him to spot the signs beforehand and make his excuses – to use his 'side door' or give reasons to leave the happy gathering *before* things turned ugly. His text books might call this a contingency, or 'damage limitation'.

His *ideal* night out was a one-to-one with Ray. It gave him a chance to offload his recent experiences on a sympathetic ear. One that knew what and who he was talking about. Central to this was the fact they had both been close to Sue. Ray was genuinely sorry to hear John's relationship with Sue had broken down. He didn't understand it He thought they were made for each other, but that's what he said about Victoria. But he was a good listener. Who else could John share all this with? As they say, 'to share a problem is to halve it'. It did help.

CHAPTER FIFTEEN

Some years later – reunited in Plymouth

"...it's *so* good to see you, John." Rose replaced the apple precisely where the stallholder had first arranged it. He remembered how neatly and precisely she did everything. Even the small things.

"But...I thought you were in -"

" - Ireland? I came back. I had to...." Her voice trailed off before she could give a full answer.

"Any special reason?" John sensed there were things he should know. Her disappearance was still unexplained; her reappearance held even more mystery. He had dreamed of this moment so many times. Of seeing her again. He had to know the truth before, as he feared, he woke up and she was gone. A second time.

"Oh I had to..." she paused, struggling to find credible reason. He remembered she screwed up her mouth when she was unsure of what she was about to say, "I had to come back for my husband." She paused once more, "My ex-husband, that is. Now."

"You were married? But you're divorced?" Immediately John knew how stupid his remark was. It was the shock. She was married and divorced in the same sentence. "This must still be one of my crazy dreams."

All he could think of was one of the last moments they had spent together – seven years ago. How it had broken their pledge.

They were having a picnic on the grass outside the Town Hall in Leicester, one warm summer's afternoon. A light breeze sent the misty spray over them from the fountains. Sparrows dined out on the remains of so many lunch boxes left behind by office workers and shop assistants. He remembered every thought, every emotion, every word. He remembered the promise that would bind them forever. Until the last. First of all they agreed they would never give themselves to anyone else. Ever.

Second there was a simple pledge. "If you die first, I want *my* heart to stop beating the second *you* pass away." They had spoken the words together, almost in perfect unison.

After each of them had made the same vow, Rose had taken out her pearl-handled clasp knife. She cut John across his palm at the end of his lifeline. Then he did the same to her. She took his hand in hers just like that first time they met when they watched the life drain out from Jessie. Then she pressed. Thin lines of blood oozed from each wound and mingled. It completed the bond never to be undone. Suddenly, he remembered where he was. In Plymouth Market. With Rose. Her voice broke his spell.

"John? Were you listening?" He had been going over the past in his mind for the thousandth time while she had been talking. The queue at the greengrocer's had grown behind them. Seven years had passed since taking that pledge in Leicester Town Hall Square - and it was still vivid. As he recalled that memory he took her hand. Her scar was still there. So was his. It was only then he noticed she wore no wedding band. The circular mark could still be seen on her ring finger. On the left hand.

That part was true, at least.

He was marvelling at how beautiful she was. Back then she was still growing into womanhood. His 'Janet Munro' he called her, named after the teen actress in the Swiss Family Robinson film. He had seen it with his parents a year or so before they met, and had been in love with the screen star ever since. He felt the same inner stirring for Rose when they first met – when she was just sixteen.

Right now the all-consuming passion he felt for her all those years ago returned. There was a scene from another film he had seen - Wuthering Heights. He remembered the words of Cathy when she realised she had lost Heathcliff. The roles were reversed now but Cathy's words came back to him with a meaning they had not held before. Cathy had said, "I *am* Heathcliff." It matched the insanity he also felt at this very moment, "I *am* Rose." Without Rose his life had meant nothing. Although he was later to feel genuine devotion to both Victoria and Sue after Rose had left him, they were eclipsed by the power that Rose had always held over him – a power he was only too willing to yield to. A power he was feeling now.

But did she feel the same? Why had she never answered his letters? Why had she taken off so suddenly back then? More to the point, what was she doing here, in Plymouth? Of all the places she could have chosen...?

Slowly, Rose withdrew her hand from his but without hesitation reached up, stroking his cheek as she had that first day by the river. She had grown just a little taller since then he thought, and was almost at eye level. Those eyes were always a misty brown but right now they seemed softer. Glistening. Vulnerable.

"It's *so* good to see you again," ("....at last," she almost added. But didn't. But he knew that's what she meant.)

"Do you live far?" He didn't wait for an answer. "I rent at the moment. Lipsom Vale. Been there just a year." His meaningless words came out without thought, denying what he had been wanting to say to her for so long.

"We live on Mannamead. Avenue. It's a second floor flat," she replied.

"We?" There was a tenseness in his voice.

"Oh, my Mum and I. Dad died." A moment's silence. "And Tilly."

"Sorry to hear about your Dad. He was a good man. Hard worker. Who is Tilly?" He feared the answer.

"She's my daughter Mathilda, named after my Gran. But we call her Tilly." She smiled as the image of her daughter appeared before her and then was gone. It had only been an hour. She was already missing her.

John could barely hide his slight uneasiness. So she had started a family. Then, conscious that they were holding up the queue at the greengrocer's he placed his hand on Rose's slender waist. He moved them both to one side. "Do you have time for a coffee? I know a nice little Italian place just round the -"

She broke in, pressing her fingers to his lips, "No." But she anticipated his disappointment by adding "You must come to ours."

Leaving him no opportunity to argue, she took his arm to lead him down Frankfurt Gate. He saw they were heading across the Western Approach footbridge leading to the multi-storey car park. There was the usual wind tunnel in "the Gate". They walked briskly but spoke very little. They exchanged glances, searching for any hint of change in each other's features – visual or otherwise.

Her car was a not-too-old, not-very-new VW Beetle. Slipping into the passenger seat evidence of Tilly was obvious. The child seat in the rear, plus early learning books gave a clue to her age. He was still determined to ask how old she was.

"She's a year behind other children at school, hence those books," came the reply but avoiding the question. It was just too vague for John's liking. They spent the rest of the journey in silence. John didn't want to distract Rose from navigating bus lanes, buses, and the impatient taxis. The flow of traffic was heavy and moved erratically from the dock area and town. They aimed towards the rail station and beyond, en route to the Mannamead area via Mutley.

Rose turned right at the end of Mutley Plain, rounding the Hyde Park pub centred in the island, then pointed the Beetle up, right, to Mannamead Road. Soon she was taking another sharp right, crossing oncoming traffic and into Mannamead Avenue. It was a cul-de-sac very familiar to him. It must have been four years ago since he was last there.

Mannamead Avenue was in a pleasant area on the fringe of the main centre of Plymouth. Surprisingly quiet, it was graced by substantial period houses hiding behind many a behind brick and stone wall, like the one where Rose had parked neatly outside. Sycamores lined the street.

"Here we are," she was taking hold of John by the arm once more as she led them through the closed front gate. The garden had hardly changed since he was there last. Rose's mother was kneeling, weeding the front border. "Look who I found." Her mother slowly got to her feet, peering over her glasses at the new arrival. They didn't have many visitors.

"John?" she said, unable to conceal her smile – that warm, genuine smile was also familiar to him.

"Molly.... Mrs Lee," he corrected himself, having immediate respect for one who he had always regarded as an ally during his time at the Gypsy Camp all those years ago in Blaby.

Molly – Mrs Lee - had the same clear eyes as Rose. This was despite spending most of her "childhood to middle age" in the harsh life afforded to the wife of a traveller. Her skin was smooth and healthy looking due to a sensible albeit frugal diet. However, her once black hair was now flecked with grey and rough hands testified to a lifetime of manual work. Next to Rose she appeared slightly shorter. That could have been due to Rose's heels. She had aged somewhat in the seven years perhaps due to grief, but she retained her young girl's smile. "How are you, John?" she asked, adding "what a blessing."

That last sentiment didn't escape John but he put it to one side as Mrs Lee led the way. They climbed the stairs to their second floor apartment. "Where's Tilly?" Rose wanted to know.

"I made her take a nap about three o'clock. It's now four so she's ready to wake up. Do you want to do it?"

Rose didn't like it when her mother left a six year old on her own but Mrs Lee had brought up three children safely on the road. She so often said there was a higher power looking out for you when all else failed. John's thoughts turned to the final moments of Rose's mare, Jessie seven years before. Then back to Rose.

Mrs Lee led John to the farmhouse-style kitchen complete with dining area. It was a different layout to the downstairs apartment he lived in as a student. He sat in the one easy chair whilst Mrs Lee put the kettle on. This gave Rose the chance to creep into the box room to find Tilly already awake, but pretending not to be. "Where's my princess?" she whispered. "She flew away!" cried Tilly, keeping herself covered by her quilt. She knew what would happen next. It was a familiar game.

After the customary tickling (by Rose) and giggling (by Tilly) the two emerged from Tilly's room quieter now, to face

the mysterious stranger. " This is your f........ errrr....my.......
friend - John - from before you were born. When Grandma and
I used to live a long, long way away. Before Daddy."

John didn't miss the sudden switch from "your" to "my", or
the reference to 'Daddy' but said nothing apart from "Hello,
Tilly."

With greetings exchanged, Mrs Lee passed around
welcome cups of tea. Tilly remained close to Rose hiding
behind her long skirt. Occasionally she would venture a peek
at the mysterious stranger when she thought he wasn't
looking.

"Well, you've become quite the handsome young man,
John."said Mrs Lee, sitting down to take Tilly onto her lap.
"You won't know this one, of course," meaning Tilly. She gave
her a squeeze, brushing her dark hair from her face.

"No," John replied, "I seem to have missed out on quite a
lot." He shot Rose a glance as if to ask 'what else do you need
to tell me?' He added, "Rose, will you show me the garden? I
always loved this house." Mrs Lee nodded her consent as she
and Rose exchanged looks before taking John downstairs to
the garden.

The one thing he did notice that was different was the
vardo at the far end of the garden. The last time he had seen it
was years ago in Blaby. "What's that all about?" he asked,
pointing to it. It was nestled under a large willow tree, next to
the stream running through the garden, underground from
the road.

"It was a condition of Mum's that, if we were to alter our
lifestyle and live in a real house, that we would bring the
vardo with us. It's now her own personal space. She meditates
there quite often, and keeps in touch with her Romany and
Celtic roots that way. She's retained some of the family
heritage too – charms and the like. We leave her to it,
although sometimes she takes Tilly in there to show her
things, just as my Gran used to do with me at her age.

Apparently the stream is the last stretch of the Devonport
Leat on its journey all the way from Princetown on the moor.
It is the purest water you can find and Mum says it enhances
her mystical powers. But don't tell anyone. Here in the city
she might be regarded a witch. You know what I mean."

They settled themselves in the pergola ready to talk more.

"How do you know this place?" she asked.

"I used to live here. In the bottom flat. When I was student. With four others." he explained. His mind drifted back to the last time he had walked round this expansive garden. He was impressed that the borders were still adorned with flowers and shrubs surrounding the manicured lawn. Unable to prevent the wry smile he recalled one special moment in that same garden.

"What's so funny?"

"I was just thinking about the last time I was here."

"When was that?" She wanted every detail.

"You won't believe this...but it was with a girl. I was perhaps nineteen or so and working part-time as barman in a nightclub. I was still at college. She was a regular, you might say, every Friday. She would turn up together with three or four of her friends.

I used to make excuses to go out to the tables to collect glasses more often than usual on those nights, just for a chance to talk to her." He paused, trying to recall what they talked about. He couldn't remember but he did remember what she looked like.

"Oh, yes...?" Rose brought him back to the present, teasing him to continue.

"Yes. We sort of connected but it never went anywhere." He wanted to avoid her reading too much into it. But he had already dug a hole for himself.

"She came here then, didn't she? To this house? What happened? What was she like...?"

"Ha!" at that point he broke into a laugh, "It was only the once. And nothing happened! But she was beautiful! She could have been a fashion model. Everyone at the night club fancied her. Lovely smiling face. I guess in some ways you two could have been sisters, what with her jet black hair and misty brown eyes and a figure to die for. Except for one thing."

"Go on then, what was that?"

He was having second thoughts about telling her but it was too late. He had to come clean. There was no going back.

"Her name was Rose, too. Rosemary, actually. " He smiled.

She demanded more. "How come nothing came of it?"

That was an easy answer. "Must have been something to do with her stupid boyfriend! He was at sea most of the time but she still remained faithful." There was silence whilst he tried to remember how he actually felt at the time, then added "...or maybe I just didn't try hard enough." Did she sense regret in his voice? Or relief? She knew which answer she wanted but didn't ask.

"You couldn't have," she said. "Just think for a moment and ask yourself why did she bother to come at all? She wouldn't have agreed to meet you here, spend at least half an hour getting ready to look her best for you, catch a bus from wherever she lived – all that just to walk round the garden with you for an hour then hop on the bus back home? It doesn't make sense. She must have been looking for something more on that afternoon. I know I would have. I think you missed a trick my lad." They both saw the funny side in this, and the truth.

"*Now* you tell me," he laughed, "she's probably married with kids now!"

"There must have been others," she was insistent, really on a mission now. "Working in a night club? All those girls?" She stopped then, seeing he was colouring up. Surely not embarrassed?

"Look. I don't think you realise. When you left so suddenly like that. Yes, I had to move on. Leaving home after what happened sometimes can make it easier to find a new life, but emotionally...." his voice trailed off.

"I'm so sorry," she gripped his arm, forcing him to face her. There were tears now. And not just hers.

"So much time wasted."

"I know." They sat in the pergola, the afternoon sun still warm on their faces. There was something she was bursting to tell him; there was something he was almost afraid to ask. One of them had to break the deadlock. They were both agonising over the same thing.

CHAPTER SIXTEEN

John learns he is a father

"Tilly. She's mine isn't she? Why didn't you tell me?" He gazed into the distance, waiting for an answer. If she was going to lie he didn't want to see it in her face. But she didn't try to deny it.

"It wasn't easy. I couldn't tell anyone. I was only just sixteen. My mother guessed but we dare not tell my Dad. It really is forbidden in Romany life. To have a child by an outsider, that is. Not that they had anything against you. You had become almost part of us. It's just that you weren't from any of the other Romany families." She found she was unusually calm at being able to tell the story at last, to the one person who really mattered. It was as important for her to tell it, as it was for him to hear. She had finally found *some* relief. But not total release. The bond they had made would never allow that, not unless they received absolution from a Romany mystic.

"You know I would have stuck by you. We could have been together, got married and - "

"Aren't you forgetting something?" she butted in, "You were still only sixteen years old. We couldn't marry without consent, and I couldn't have a child without being married. You had your dreams. Your ambitions to be an engineer. I couldn't spoil that for you. It wouldn't have been fair."

"Fair?" he couldn't hide his disappointment. She seemed blind to his position, "What's fair about not knowing I had a daughter?"

She remained silent. Rose knew he was right. She also knew she had to think of Tilly. In her mind the two reasons cancelled each other out.

"When did you get married? Before or after the baby?" He wasn't sure why it was so important. He just felt compelled to ask. He had to know.

"It was before. I was less than three months gone. Sean was just a boy I had been promised to, a long time before I met you. Those pre-arrangements still existed, especially between

Romany families with ties stretching back decades. My Dad and his both worked together. Sean lived out towards Dunton Bassett. Over the years our two families had even struck camp together. We were more like cousins."

"Didn't he suspect that it wasn't his? When you started to show?"

"Thanks to my mother we managed to keep it a secret early on - as much from my Dad as from Sean. In our custom we can marry at short notice without too much fuss if it's been pre-arranged. We had our own ceremony after which the union was blessed in Blaby church. We went to live in Dunton Bassett, all together in one camp. Sean was working on the road construction with his Dad and mine. They had moved site up towards Lutterworth and Rugby anyway.

As soon as it seemed right we told everyone I was pregnant. After a while, my mother convinced Sean and my Dad that it might be better if she, my Gran and I went back to her sister in Ireland. They agreed that I should be able to have the baby there more comfortably. Her sister lived in a permanent camp. There were at least two mid-wives readily on hand as well."

"But when Tilly was born he must have known that that you were already pregnant before you got married?" John was calmer, and posed it as a question rather than an accusation. Rose was ready with the answer.

"That part was easy. As you can imagine, we are a very closed community in Ireland. There was not much contact between English and Irish Romanies. When Tilly was born we still kept her a secret from the outside world for several weeks afterwards, before registering her and getting a certificate. Only then did we tell Sean. He never suspected."

"Then you came back to England?" John waited for her to continue.

"Yes. Sean was delighted to be a father. By that time he had his own vardo. I think my Dad and his helped to buy it. That was their secret from my Mum and me this time. They did a lot of things together outside of work. Sean was working hard and making good money. But both his and my Dad died suddenly and there was little keeping us there. Sean's Mum went back to Ireland but my Mum stayed with us. There were still so many painful memories there for him, for his Mum, and for my Mum. As well as for me. Then a chance came up for him to move to a new site in Plymouth, so he took it. We all needed a fresh start anyway. It was the company, Peter Lundstrom, who found us this flat. They even paid for relocation expenses – including bringing the vardo down!

Having a fixed address for the first time was amazing. It was a novelty for all of us but we settled in surprisingly well. It was quite a treat not having to collect wood for the fire, or water from the nearby stream. At last we could each have our own room, our own space. Not that we had many possessions to bring with us. We didn't have a great number of clothes.

Buying a lot of food in one go and keeping it in a fridge took a bit of getting used to. Quite a change from having rabbits and pheasant hanging – in what would have to have been the kitchen. Best of all, we had never been so clean. Of course we had always washed – Mum was very keen to make sure we did, even if sometimes it had to be outdoors – but to have a hot shower or long soak in the bath was pure luxury.

I was pleased in other ways, too. Romany life and always living outdoors was taking its toll on Mum, plus I felt better about Tilly going to the same school without having to uproot her every few months. Sean had learnt to drive by this time so he bought an old Vauxhall to get to work. It also meant we could get about more. Mum loved it. We all did. We were settled again and it helped Sean – and Mum – get over their loss. Me too, I still miss my Dad.

Sean took to his new job well. When our fathers were alive they tended to protect him or to think for him. Without them to turn to he had to stand on his own two feet more. His bosses noticed this and he was given more responsibility. He responded well to that too and it gave him more confidence. He became a lot happier and it helped him even more to get over losing his Dad. Even so after a while Sean and I admitted to each other there was something missing in our lives. Tilly was growing up daily but she was the only thing keeping us together. He knew something wasn't right but couldn't fathom it out. After all, we had everything we had ever dreamed of. Almost. I knew what my problem was. Mum guessed it too." With that she grasped his arm tightly. With both hands. She didn't have to say what it was.

"I couldn't forget you either." He was speaking for both of them.

"Rose?" John? Are you two staying out there all evening? I have tea ready." It was her mother calling. "You're staying for something to eat, aren't you, John?"

Rose nodded to him her approval but it was John who answered, "Yes please. That would be very kind."

Only then did John realise how hungry he was and the meal *was* truly delicious. Hotpot – his favourite out of all Mrs Lee's specialities. He was hardly surprised at the choice and guessed it was inspired by camp fire cooking. He did wonder, though, how Mrs Lee managed to get hold of substitutes for the herbs and plants she used to find in the wild. The ingredients certainly were not straight out of a packet off the supermarket shelves.

Over the course of the meal Tilly settled down to John being there, even to the point of telling him about her days at school, who her best friend was, and how much she missed Daddy. That last notion struck home with John. As soon as they had finished eating, and after a token offer to wash up and being refused, he made excuses that he had to get back. But to what? He was loving it there.

"I'll walk you to the door," said Rose as he was saying his goodbyes, first to Tilly, with a wave, and then to Mrs Lee, with a hug. He didn't complain when she held onto him just a little longer than he had expected.

He was even more surprised at her parting words, "I'm sorry that we interfered."

He was surprised, but he understood. Rose and her family had literally upped sticks and left overnight and unexpectedly that summer. But it was the lack of reply to his letters that was unexplainable. As he was soon to learn, Rose's parents intercepted them without her knowing. He had addressed them in an outer envelope to her father, care of the company site office where he worked. He couldn't do anything else. After three letters, he gave up.

Her Mum had kept them though, handing them over to her

after her Dad had died. Rose explained how they had broken her heart on reading them. He had poured out his own heart on those pages and it was then she realised that his heart was breaking too, letter by letter. She knew she had made a mistake at the time and here was the proof to punish her all over again, but then it was too late. She was resolved there and then to find him again, no matter how long it took, although her responsibilities to Tilly still counted most over all other considerations. But that did not stop the need for John's presence with her, the bond they had, resurfacing in her quieter moments, relentlessly.

Leaving the warmth of the kitchen and anticipating a chill in the early evening air, he buttoned up his jacket as they reached the bottom of the stairs. Rose slipped a coat around her shoulders. Once out into the fresh air and without a single word she placed both hands on his shoulders. She made the first moved, kissing him gently before moulding herself into him, partly for comfort, partly for warmth. Being able to hold each other was all they needed right now. Neither spoke. They were en-wrapped as closely in their thoughts as they were physically to each other.

Reluctantly she released him before taking both his hands in hers, pressing them to her cheek. "I did look for you even after I was married. I wanted to to tell you about...to let you see....Tilly. But by that time you had started college and moved away. With your parents. To the Isle of Wight. Or Southampton I suppose it was. I had to give you up and didn't have any choice, for Tilly's sake. But I never did forget you or give you up inside here." She pointed to her heart.

"How did your Dad die? That's when you moved down here wasn't it?"

"Heart attack. He'd been having regular pains but he kept on working. Then one day unloading a lorry load of cement he simply collapsed. That's what I was told anyway." She went on. "That changed everything. Dad never let Mum work. It was his job to provide. But with his going like that it meant she was on her own. There was *some* money saved but it wasn't nearly enough. That's when Sean was offered a job down here and we all moved to Plymouth. We agreed that Mum should look after Tilly while I went off to work. That way I could look after my mother financially. Sean was very good about it.

Even though my schooling over the years had been a bit, well, hit and miss, I did manage to get a job in an office. I could type and my English wasn't bad. It was an insurance firm. The people I worked with were very friendly and kind. If they knew I was a Romany they never let on. It was different from staying at home all the while or living in a closed community. Some nights I would even go out into the town with some of the girls. Sean was OK about it, given that he often went for a pint with his work mates, or go to watch the Argyle football game. Being with other girls, and those of a similar age, taught me what clothes to wear, that sort of things. I will always be a Romany, but I was changing.

Soon I found that through having to draft out all the letters and policies for the underwriters, I was automatically beginning to learn about the business. It seemed quite interesting. Eventually I asked if *I* could train as an underwriter. They said 'yes' so I studied hard and even took exams. I passed and I'm now officially a "professional". She laughed at this.

They both did. It was then he understood how – why – she was a lot more sophisticated than she had been as a Romany girl. It did show in her dress sense as well as her manner. How she spoke and carried herself. Back then she dressed in jumpers knitted by her grandmother or hand-me-down skirts and dresses altered, courtesy of her mother. Her Wellington boots were now replaced by heels and designer labels. But underneath all that she was the same Rose. It was the way she looked at him, knew what he was thinking.

Rose continued her story. Now that she had started to unburden herself of all the waste of the missing years she wanted it all to be told - to get it all out there so they could move on. "The more I grew in confidence in my job, the less I relied on Sean. That was the beginning of the end I suppose. We rarely argued which, in itself was a sign that our lives were going in different directions. I guess it's only when you share common interests that you then leave yourselves open to disagree about parts of them. Apart from our being Romanies we were becoming quite different individuals. But it wasn't just me who was changing. Sean was no longer under the influence of his parents, or ruled by life in a gypsy camp. He also found that he, too, fitted in well with his work mates. Of course life as a construction worker is much different from that of an insurance clerk.

One day we simply sat down and talked about it calmly and sensibly. Tilly was central to most of our concerns. Once we had sorted that out in our own minds, with Mum playing her part and Sean given free and regular access to Tilly, *we* started to make new plans. The hardest part – especially for him and Tilly - was his moving out. I worked out that I could manage to keep the flat without being too dependant on Sean financially. That meant that he could get a place, which he found - sharing with some work mates, near Exeter. We had to go through a kind of separation in any case. There was no unfaithfulness, mental or physical abuse so all we had to do was to prove that we were not 'man and wife' for two years. Then the divorce became final. That was only a few months ago. Now I'm pretty much free to do what I want, outside of ensuring a stable home for Tilly and Mum. That's about it, really. What are you doing now, anyway?" she wanted to know.

"I completed my course in Southampton and then Plymouth, passed my Finals and got a job with Peter Lundstrom. Building motorways, as a surveyor. I had already spent a gap year with them half way through the course, on-the-job training. They offered me a provisional job for when I was qualified. I applied, and they sent me down here, on the Devon Expressway."

CHAPTER SEVENTEEN

John and Rose plan to see each other again

He finished the account of all that he could remember when he suddenly realised where he was - where *both of them* were. He was back in the garden of the flat he used to rent in Mannamead Avenue as a student. All those years between melted away but there was one thing Rose wanted to know most of all. "I'm glad you found Jessie's name plate. Did you figure out what my message was?"

He did, *and* he remembered their vow, "If you die first," he said, his eyes fixed upon hers, "I want *my* heart to stop beating the second *you* pass away."

"But if *you* die first," she replied, "I want my heart to stop beating the second *you* pass away."

Back then seven years ago he didn't immediately guess the meaning of the sign she had left - Jessie's name plate. It contradicted what he had just read in the letter pushed through his door when he returned from Southampton. But now he thought it could have been something his Mum had made her write – not her words.

Now it all became clear. They were one again. Their faces were pressed gently together, his tears mingling with hers. It reminded him of the way their blood had run together to bind them when he and Rose had cut their love lines, the time outside the Town Hall in Leicester. That first yet final summer together. It bound them together all over again. They stood in the garden in silence now, the pledge they had made repeating over and over in their heads.

"Rose? John?" It was her mother. How long had they been in the garden? "It's gone seven o'clock. We need to get Tilly ready for bed. Are you going to drive John home first?"

"No. I'm fine. I'll walk."

"Are you sure?"

"Yes. I need to clear my head anyway. The night air will help. I'm only a mile away." He looked up to the window just as Mrs Lee closed it.

Rose drew John closer to kiss him with the true depth of her love. She turned on her heels, skipping across the gravel path and inside. His eyes followed her, rewarded by her brief turn to wave as she reached the door. He raised his hand in reply, but she was already gone. He replaced the hand in his coat pocket.

There was a note she must have slipped inside when he was distracted. 'Call me. Soon. X X X' followed by her number.

He couldn't remember much about the walk home. Why should he? Of course it was a familiar route to him, turning left at the end of the close and heading towards Mutley Plain. The Hyde Park pub came into view. It always seemed a strange sight stood as it was, marooned in the centre of a traffic island. He did notice the warmth of its lounge lights, though, casting a soft glow across the pavement. "That used to be my local," he mused.

With all the shops closed there weren't many others out at that time, either strolling into town, or doing a late night shop at the Gateway supermarket, or even Coopers' Off Licence. Some must have been on their way home, like him. Anyone waiting for a bus would be going towards Home Park and beyond, even to Saltash, or in the opposite direction into the town centre. But Lipsom Vale, where he rented, was off the main bus routes but quieter because of it, so he had to walk anyway. He guessed some might be early diners arriving at the Greek restaurant opposite Gateways. It was there the first time he had ever savoured stuffed vine leaves. He could taste them now even though he was still full from the substantial – too substantial – tea he had enjoyed two hours earlier.

Crossing the park leading finally to his house on Salcombe Road, he noticed how peaceful it was. Although dark now, every few yards the park lights marked his path home. They looked like they could be the original Victorian lamp posts, their lamps converted from gas to electric in the 1950's. What a story they could tell. How many clandestine meetings had they witnessed under their soft gaslight?

Obviously they had been spared the ravages of the bombing of the city in the war. That's what he had come to like about Plymouth, the heritage it still managed to retain.

This contrasted sharply with the already dated concrete monstrosities that made up the post-war rebuilding of the shopping centre and council offices. They simply had no character. In spite of his path being well lit, he could still make out the moon and stars filtering through the light cloud overhead. It fitted his mood perfectly.

The last time he had walked across the park in the dark like this it had been much later – around midnight in fact. It was winter but the stars were just as bright – perhaps brighter, or was that his imagination. He remembered it clearly, and the peace he had felt at the time. It was with a girl, and a pretty one at that.

But the only reason he remembered that was that she had reminded him of Rose. It would be barely three years then since he had left Blaby. The memory of those final days of that summer were still raw. He couldn't think of the girl's name, not surprising as he wasn't going out with her or anything. She was the girlfriend of the captain of the college soccer team he played for. *His* name was Dai, that he *did* remember. And it *was* all so innocent. They were all at a party somewhere off Mutley Plain and she wanted to leave. Dai didn't. But knowing he could trust John, he asked him to walk his girlfriend home.

John agreed, not just because of her similarity to Rose, but because he just enjoyed the idea of a walk home with a girl, no strings attached, and to be able to talk *about* Rose. The memories of the break-up had been building up inside him again for several weeks previously, and it somehow made it easier for him to open up *because* he didn't really know Dai's girlfriend.

As it turned out she didn't seem to mind anyway. She had one or two things she wanted to share too, about Dai. She and Dai had been together for two years and before college, in Swansea. They lived just round the corner from him so he didn't have to double back far.

Reaching her front door, he waited until she was nearly inside before he turned, waved goodbye and said, "Thank you."

"You too." she said, "I hope it works out for you. Don't give up."

A phone ringing in the distance brought him back to his senses and to where he was. He was still a few yards from his front door but he could tell it was his phone. He hurriedly searched for his keys. Before the impatient caller hung up John was inside, snatching up the phone. "Did you run all the way?" It was Rose.

"It's closer than you think....how did you know my number?"

"Not from you, thank you very much. Isn't it normal to ask a girl for her number on the first date?" She laughed. "Luckily you're in *New Numbers*."

"*New Numbers*? What did she mean?"

"It came through the door yesterday."

Then he remembered. The Post Office sent out updates every so often in between the main phone directory, just providing the numbers for recent subscribers. He noticed his own copy lying next to the phone underneath some mail, as he spoke.

"I'm so glad we found each other again. It's like a dream." He let her talk on. Clearly she needed to. He was content just to listen. "My Mum in particular is....well....relieved. She just couldn't stop talking about you. Apparently she had a confession to make to me. To both of us. The guilt she felt when we first had to leave for Ireland all those years ago has weighed heavily on her ever since. She hid it well, until now when you turned up. Then it was more than she could stand. She saw how well you had turned out; she knew there was always something eating me up inside ever since...we left you; she couldn't stand it any more. She was never quite sure that she and Dad did the right thing making me give you up. It was like her confession. She even disappeared into her vardo sometimes, just to pray for you. I suspect for both of us, too.

Mum accepted Sean in a way, but she could see that he and I weren't the same. Not the same as you and I used to be together. Not the way we are now. Today brought it all back to her. She had to admit she was wrong. I was wrong too. I am so sorry, John, but Tilly has always been my first concern. Tilly misses her Dad of course She keeps asking where he is, but not as much as I thought she would. Mum, me, Tilly – we have fallen into a new routine. Things have been working out quite well."

"And then I turned up."

But Rose wasn't finished yet. "Not at all! Are you free tomorrow? Mum always goes to church in the morning and takes Tilly with her for Sunday School. It gives me the chance to get up slowly and have breakfast before they get back. We don't usually have our main meal until tea-time. We could all go out together before then. It would give you time to get to know... your daughter."

"My daughter," he pondered. It was something he was struggling to get used to. How long had it been since he'd been a father? Four hours? He definitely wanted to see her, and his family, tomorrow. "Shall I pick you up about 11 o'clock?"

"Can you make it earlier? We can have some you-and-me time. Alone."

"10.30 it is."

"No later."

"OK. 10.30 or earlier."

"I'd better go," she whispered, Mum's turned off the TV ready to go to bed. Good night... love you."

"I never stopped," he said, replacing the phone on the receiver. Rose was still standing motionless at the other end of the phone, taking in the sadness surrounding what he had just said.

CHAPTER EIGHTEEN

John shocked to being a family man – and another surprise

John's alarm was set for 8 o'clock that Sunday morning. Early for him. Too early, but it would give him time to clean out – or rather empty out – his Land Rover. That would be plenty of time to make it for 10.30 at Rose's. As excited as he was at the prospect of a day out with his new family, he still had to force himself out of bed.

The events of the previous day made him feel "wired" long after he put the phone down. It must have been 3.00 am before he finally went to sleep. He watched the hours slowly tick by whilst he went over and over in his head every word they had said. He examined every thought they shared, every new revelation. At last he had the chance to uncover the true story behind the missing years. There was much more to discover and he couldn't wait.

He combined breakfast – toast and coffee – with cleaning his car. It was so unusual for him to be up so early on a Sunday. Casual remarks from passing neighbours reminded him of the fact. "Got a hot date, John? Bit early for you." quipped the guy next door. If only he knew!

But it typified what a pleasant area Lipsom Vale was and why he chosen this particular part of Plymouth. Because his assignment on that section of the A38 was temporary, he had taken a two year lease on his end-terraced house with a six month break. His job with Peter Lundstrom was permanent, but he had to be prepared to move anywhere, at any time. So he rented.

Soon after 10 o'clock he found himself locking his front door and going through his mental checklist. He would suggest they drove to the moors, perhaps for a picnic. Always the organiser, he listed flask, sandwiches, coat (waterproof, just in case), decent walking shoes, blanket – plus a compass.

He started out for the flat. Traffic was not too bad getting onto North Hill and along Mutley Plain so he made good time to Mannamead Avenue. He was ten minutes earlier than promised but Rose was already at the window as he pulled up to the house. This time the gate was open so he parked in the drive.

They met at the front door and wrapped their arms around each other. "So it wasn't a dream," she said. They stood looking at each other in silence. "Come inside," she said finally. They turned to climb up the stairs into the kitchen. "Coffee?"

"No. I've just had one. Thanks."

She led him to the sofa in the area just off the kitchen. "How did you sleep?"

"I didn't. Not until gone three at least."

"Me neither. There was a lot to think about. I had to force myself not to call you again." She paused. "So how do you feel about being a family man?"

"It would have been nicer to have known about it sooner," he said. Then, realising it came over a little harsh, a little unfair, he added. "Sorry. It must have been hard for you. I just wish I could have been there to help. But what I really would have liked... why didn't you simply come to me that summer as soon as you found out, and say 'We're going to have a baby'."

"You have to believe me that's all I wanted too. But I was so young. So confused. I loved you so much that I was worried I was ruining things for you. Placing you in a trap. You had such a life ahead of you. Such promise. And I was frightened. I had broken the rules that we Romany families live by and I was terrified at what might happen to me. I did confide in my Mum. Luckily she understood and helped me through it. The rest you know.

Mum was amazing of course. She was so fond of you, although I know she never said. She was the one level-headed person I so desperately needed at that time. She helped me every step of the way – the marriage arrangements, later on making sure I was in the best care to have the baby, even ensuring my Dad, Sean and his family, never suspected. Everyone on both sides of the family just fitted in and carried on as normal after the arrival of Tilly. You might say life *was* normal for them. But I wish you could have been there. Do you want to see some photographs? There aren't many -"

Rose had them already prepared on the sideboard. Although they were in black and white they were clear and captured the christening of Tilly perfectly. All the family gathered around - and, of course, Sean. John focussed as much on Sean as he did Tilly, noticing his build of a typical manual worker. He was tall and, much to his disappointment, quite a decent looking bloke. "He looks OK."

"Yes he was, is, really. He always provided well for us. Especially after Dad passed away leaving Mum on her own." Rose was keen to change the subject. "What do you have planned for us? For today?" (But John was thinking 'For the rest of our lives...' It had crossed Rose's mind too.)

"I thought we might take a ride over Dartmoor. Perhaps even take in Princetown. I've made sandwiches for us. And a flask. We could have a picnic. There are plenty of walks there or on the way, say around Burrator Reservoir. There's a very popular pub there. In Princetown. The Plume of Feathers. Trouble is it gets packed on Sunday lunchtime. There's a group calling themselves The Pheasant Pluckers who lead a sing-along. Loads of students from Plymouth tend to go there. I used to drop in some Sundays. We may have to settle for a table on the lawn, especially with Tilly."

"That sounds fun. It will be a lovely change for Mum.... and Tilly..... ." She paused. "Hold me, John. They'll be back soon." He took her in his arms and kissed her. She was *so* beautiful! He had dreamt of this moment so many times.

Being alone together was all they wanted at that moment. To share valuable minutes – just the two of them – almost hoping that Tilly and her grandmother would be late back, perhaps caught up in conversation with a fellow church-goer. Or maybe the priest had decided on an extra long service. But it was not to be. "Mummy! We're home!" It was Tilly, bursting in and stomping up the stairs. "Guess who we saw in church... Daddy!" The blood drained from John's face as there he stood in the doorway to the kitchen. It was Sean.

"Hello Rose. How are you? Did you forget?" She had. It was *his* weekend to have Tilly. Surprised and shocked, she struggled to find the right words.

"Oh...I...errrr...so much has happened. Is it? *This* weekend? Yes.... sorry... it's been a busy week. Ummmm... this is my..... friend.... John... from when we used to live in Blaby." She hurried to put the kettle on. To buy time and to collect her thoughts. Mrs Lee went over to help, exchanging whispers with her daughter.

"Pleased to meet you," said John, extending his hand to shake Sean's.

"You too," said Sean. They shook hands. They fell silent again, pretending to be preoccupied by what the girls were busying themselves doing at the sink.

Tilly broke the ice. "Let me show you what I drew at school, Daddy." She led Sean to her room.

That gave Rose the chance to explain to John, in a half whisper, that she was sorry but had totally forgotten Sean always had Tilly every fourth Sunday. John could only wonder about her introduction of him to Sean. He had been relegated from lover to friend in less than a minute. But he latched on quickly and went along with it. He agreed to keep his distance, on the surface at least. That also meant physical distancing for the moment until they had sorted things out. In some ways it should not matter if Sean and Rose were divorced. But he appreciated that they all had Tilly to think about. She could easily be confused and upset unless they were very careful.

Rose and John put some space between them as they heard Sean and Tilly coming out of her room. "What are you chaps up to today?" asked Sean.

"We planned a trip to the moors, perhaps take in Princetown."

Tilly jumped in quickly. "Will you come too, Daddy? Pleeee-ase!"

"Yes. You must, Sean." It was John, shooting Rose a quick glance as if to say, 'What else could I do?'

"Oh, no. I couldn't," said Sean, but Rose agreed, "Of course you must. That's right, isn't it Mum?"

With everyone so insistent Sean looked down at Tilly, smiling, "OK... looks like I have no choice. Shall we use my car?"

"We can all fit in mine," said John. "There's plenty of room."

John's food supplies for the trip were quickly boosted to accommodate another mouth to feed. Ensuring everyone had adequate clothing for the uncertainty of moorland weather – and sensible walking shoes – Mrs Lee ushered everyone downstairs to load into John's Land Rover.

"Nice wheels, John." said Sean.

"Oh, I don't own it. It's my company vehicle. I need an off-roader for my job."

"Who do you work for?"

"Peter Lundstrom. Building the new motorway. I'm a surveyor. And you Sean?"

"This you won't believe. I work for Peter Lundstrom too."

"You're joking. As what?"

"I'm a pipe layer. But I'm on the section further up the line. Just outside Exeter. My company vehicle is a dumper truck. Mine is this heap here." Sean pointed to his beat up Fiesta.

"Why don't you sit in the front?" John felt this was the best all round. He didn't really want Mrs Lee next to him. That would have meant Tilly, Rose and Sean getting cosy in the back, something he definitely did not want. Rose couldn't sit next to him without raising suspicions.

The route onto the moors posed no problems as far as traffic. They had no city congestion to contend with. It was just families taking advantage of the fine weather and doing pretty much the same as they were. Savouring the joys of living so close to open space and clean air.

Tilly chattered away to Mrs Lee and Rose in the back, explaining the story they had been told by the Sunday school teacher while the grown-ups, including Mrs Lee, took the more sombre service. Rose asked Tilly to talk more quietly. This was not so much because Tilly *was* loud, but she couldn't hear what Sean and John were talking about in the front. Rose hardly expected them both to get on so well, and wasn't quite sure whether she was pleased or felt uncomfortable about it. Maybe a little jealous?

In the end her curiosity became too much, "What are you two boys talking about?" Tilly stopped talking, as eager now as Rose was to hear the answer.

"Oh, just work stuff," was Sean's reply, "nothing to interest you." They grinned at each other and carried on talking. The girls remained silent. Listening.

It was a pleasant drive as they reached the cattle grid to signify they had reached the official start to Dartmoor. The two men continued swapping lies. They knew their every word was being recorded for future questioning so they loaded it with deliberate exaggerations, not exactly lies. After half an hour they approached Burrator Reservoir. "Ready for our first stopover?" said John, turning his head slightly to invite response from the passengers on the back seat. The reply was a unanimous, 'Yes.'

Entering the reservoir Tilly was excited to see the ponies grazing near to the car park, attracted by visitors feeding them. Strictly against the rules of the National Park, of course. She ran towards them. Naturally, they scattered into the nearby woods much to her disappointment.

As the party started out on their walk around the water itself, Rose and Mrs Lee let Sean take over with Tilly. It was his time after all, and gave Rose and John legitimate reason to walk together chatting between themselves. Mrs Lee kept a respectful distance, keeping her eye on the capers of Sean and Tilly but pleased that they still got on so well despite the divorce.

The weather kept dry and sunny so the blanket was spread over a clean patch of grass and the picnic laid out. It was several hours since breakfast they all tucked in heartily, especially Sean who had missed the first meal of the day. Getting up later than he had meant to, he had to drive at top speed down from Tiverton to make sure he made the church for the service. Not that he was over religious, but he wanted to see Tilly at Sunday school. He paid little attention to the actual service, instead he had stared through the glass partition to where the children's class took place.

With the feasting over and some remnants left for Tilly to feed the ducks, they packed up and continued their walk back to the Land Rover. "Looks like Princetown is off the cards today, " said John. "Look at that mist coming down over the rise."

Princetown was about a 15 minutes drive away and they

knew that, by the time they reached the village, it would be shrouded in dense mist. Typical of the moorland climate, the weather could change very quickly. They had noticed the slender fingers of mist snaking down slowly over the nearby tor and into the valley beneath, creeping towards them. Ten minutes later the tor and the road into Princetown were completely shrouded.

They had considered exploring the Foxtor Mires but that was definitely too dangerous to contemplate unless there was full visibility. Even Dartmoor ponies could be victim to the bogs if they strayed from the well-worn tracks through the 'Quakers'. That was what the locals called the matting of bright green mosses that covered the surfaces of the bogs. Underneath the surface the depth could be over six feet. Enough to drown a man even. The reason they were called 'Quakers' was because if you stepped on the edge of these expanses, a whole area stretching several yards wide and across would 'quake' or tremble. That showed where *not* to walk.

"OK, same seating arrangements as before, looks like we're on our way home." John was ready for a further catch up with Sean about progress at the Exeter site. As it turned out Sean was not just a pipe layer, but a 'ganger' - in other words a kind of foreman. He was overseeing the gangs of men working in pairs either laying the pipes or as labourers for them, and who had to provide enough pipes and "compo" (cement mix) so that the actual pipe layers never ran out. Run out of materials and the laying of pipes was held up leading to slow progress and no bonus. Of course John knew all this because he had to survey the line of the trench (for the drainage pipes) as well as the depth and fall so that the water drained away properly. He and Sean had a lot in common.

Sean also had responsibilities for health and safety, first aid, hiring and firing. It was mainly the latter, with quite a few Irish workers seeking better pay and a better life. While he was attached to the Exeter site and John to Plymouth, their paths had not yet crossed. That could soon change as the two sections of the motorway would eventual join up.

Arriving back at Mannamead Avenue later on that afternoon the party were in good spirits. Rose and Mrs Lee were relieved that the surprise turn-up of Sean had worked out so well, after the initial awkwardness for Rose and John. Mrs Lee was keen to get into her kitchen to prepare a late tea, whilst Tilly still had plenty of energy – demanding that her Dad sit with her in the garden while she read from one of her early learning books.

John and Rose were grateful for more time to themselves, if only to relax watching TV and chatting generally about their lives. Inevitably this involved them asking whether or not they were seeing anyone else. They both declared themselves free, to their mutual relief.

Half an hour later Tilly returned with Sean in tow. Mrs Lee asked if he would like to stay for tea, which he declined. It was nearing Tilly's bedtime anyway and Sean made excuses that he had an early start on Monday. He said his goodbyes, with a warm handshake for John, and a promise to see them in a few weeks time.

John decided to leave shortly after – again so that Tilly could settle herself properly before getting ready for bed.

"Call me tomorrow evening?" He promised Rose he would as he kissed her one final time before climbing into his Land Rover, reflecting on the day's events as the wheels of the four-by-four crunched over the gravel drive.

They failed to notice Tilly, peeking out from behind the curtain in an upstairs window.

The long conversations he had with Sean made him reflect on all that had gone on in his life the year or so immediately prior to bumping into Rose the day before. John had made friends with several of his co-workers from Ireland. He loved the way they were generous spirited and passionate about all they did, at work and at play. He would have to share all that with Rose one day.

But first his thoughts turned back to what Sean had been telling him that afternoon.

As far as hiring and firing was concerned, Sean was doing

more hiring than firing. John had noticed that the number of workers from Ireland seemed to be growing at both sites, Exeter and Plymouth. The influx of Irish "navvies" - navigators – was customary in the construction business. In the 19th century, first the building of the canals and then the railways led to a mass "import" of labour from both sides of the Irish border.

The need to strengthen the road network in post-war Britain created another demand for skilled manual labour. Doubtless the recent increase in civil unrest was a factor contributing to a little more than usual level of arrivals from Ireland.

'The English' as they were referred to by some of the Irish, found it quite amusing that whole clusters of workers within the gangs seemed to know each other beforehand. The main reason was that the Irish contingent was mainly comprised of brothers, fathers and sons, cousins and distant cousins, or just friends coming over who originated from the same area. It helped them to settle in easier and quicker.

Occasionally you could backfire, if they came over nursing 'old enmities', but normally it was a peaceful exodus.

Another amazing thing – and John agreed – was that the Irish guys genuinely got on well with 'the English'. They never seemed to stick together to the *exclusion* of English workers, or of those from any other background. Not only were they tremendously hard-working but they seemed to compete with each other on occasion. It could be on how many bricks or blocks were laid, or nine- inch porous pipes, or the quality as well as yardage of tarmac laid. In spirit and dedication they were as "professional" as surveyors and civil engineers, even without formal qualifications.

This loyalty to the job was matched by their loyalty to each other. John witnessed this at first hand. When he was first in Plymouth and still on his surveying course, he had a student network to rely on for finding a place to live.

He didn't have this when he returned for the second time to take up a permanent job at Peter Lundstrom, but new Irish friends he had made on site soon compensated for that...

CHAPTER NINETEEN

Rose and John start to plan a new beginning

With a place of his own John was able to settle well back into his life in Plymouth without too many distractions. He threw his energies into his day to day responsibilities as a surveyor on the Expressway. He did keep in contact with Ray, though, and sometimes Ray and Bren together - out of working hours. That kept him grounded as well as ensuring it wasn't 'all work and no play'.

Occasionally the subject of Sue would be come up when he was on his own with Ray. After John shared all that had happened with Sue during those final days in Teignmouth, it was Ray who decided to keep in touch with her. John didn't mind. He was even relieved. That way he remained posted on how she was getting on without complicating matters. Emotions might still remain raw between himself and Sue. He did learn that her Mum had passed away not long after their split. He sent his condolences and flowers to her funeral with a brief note.

She responded with a 'thank you' letter together with an update, saying that she would be resuming her nursing training – but at Exeter – with the aim to return to Teignmouth and the Community Hospital, as soon as a position became available. She was living in her Mum's house now and thanked him for 'saving' it from the bulldozers, now that work had started on the town bypass. It put his mind at rest.

John had already settled back into his new life for a few months before his unexpected encounter with Rose again. Prior to that they were difficult, lonely days but necessary in some ways. It enabled the healing process after his break up with Sue to run its course, and Victoria had gone back to Cornwall by this stage so that also presented no problems. You could say that the reappearance of Rose in his life was perfectly timed. He had never really forgotten her, but re-establishing some stability into his life meant that he could take in their chance meeting whilst retaining his sanity. In his darkest moments he was concerned about how irrational his thoughts were sometimes. Even after seven years he was still haunted by all that had happened that last summer in Blaby.

Having his own place fitted in perfectly for new reasons now. It meant they could plan proper 'just me and you time' with Rose fairly regularly. Often this involved a sleep-over for Rose, and sometimes for Tilly *and* Rose as long as it was a weekend. Very soon Rose started to introduce her stamp on the place with little touches here and there, such as new curtains and cushions and such. Best of all, though, it was in the kitchen that the situation really improved. Living life as a bachelor led John to a typically bland diet, rarely changing. Rose brought in a new dimension to that, not a Romany influence, necessarily, but she shared recipes with some of the girls at work and used John as her guinea pig. He didn't mind a bit.

Sean visited on the agreed weekends to see Tilly, the dates firmly in Rose's diary now. That gave them even more opportunities to spend time alone. By now he knew about Rose and John. When Sean could manage a two-day weekend, quite often he would stay over at Rose's flat on a sleep-over, which Tilly loved. Rose could then stay over at John's, happy that her Mum had adult company and Sean could have a more relaxing weekend with undivided attention for his daughter. These arrangements worked out even better once Sean had *his* own place near Exeter. Tilly was now able to grow up against a stable and loving background once again.

If Sean could get an extra day off at a weekend, and Tilly didn't have a school night, grandma and grandchild would be treated to a 'holiday' with Sean, staying over at his place. Mrs Lee rarely had a break away, apart from the occasional visit to relatives in Ireland, so it suited everybody. It also meant that Sean could enjoy proper meals, courtesy of his ex-mother in law, something he *did* miss. He had to give up his bed to them whilst he had the couch, but it was a fair compromise.

With seven years to catch up on, John and Rose were never short of things to talk about. Neither of them were the same innocents that they were in those first days in Blaby. John less so than Rose, as she had only ever known the two men. John was out of choice, Sean out of necessity, but she had tried to be a proper wife to him.

Now their thoughts often turned to getting married. Their caution only rested with their need to respect how Tilly might react. She still loved her father, whilst John was still looked upon as a family friend, albeit a pretty constant one.

The fact that Rose had integrated into what you might call 'normal society' since they were last together did make things easier. Rose and Sean had faced that transition on their own, but with success. Tilly hardly thought about it, accepting the new life as normal since she barely remembered their Romany days.

It was Mrs Lee who found it the hardest, but the new comforts of living in a real house went a long way in helping her to adjust. At first she would not step out the front door to go shopping without Rose, but she soon became used to it, relishing her new freedom. The friendliness of Mutley Plain overcame most of her fears of the unknown, being an ideal stepping stone before venturing into 'the big city'.

Her other refuge was her vardo. It allowed her to keep in touch with her lifelong traditions, keeping faith with the old ways. Often she might rely on them to overcome minor troubles in their lives, or illnesses, by meditation and connecting with the energies brought to her via the water running under its wheels. She also prayed for them all.

"John, why don't you write a journal?" asked Rose, one day when they were chilling out. They were curled up on the sofa at his place, she flicking through a magazine, he not really watching the TV.

"Oh, I don't know. What would I write about?"

"Whatever you like," she said. "You could go back to before you met me. Do you remember all those tales you used to tell me about growing up in Blaby, living out in the country, and all that?"

"I don't know. Who'd be interested?"

"I would, for one. And it could be something for Tilly to read one day. If we're going to make this permanent, she'll need to know *all* about you." She was clearly leading up something.

"So, this 'permanent' thing might be -?"

"- you, me – and Tilly – moving in together."

"Getting married?" He noticed how she paused before she answered, but not too long.

"OK. If you insist." They both laughed at this. "Is that a proposal?"

"I suppose it is, but you started it, Rose."

"Then you'd better finish it," she replied, moving even closer, to kiss him. "Mum would love it too."

He pulled away to see what expression she had on her face. "Now hold on. Let's talk about this. Perhaps we need to draw up a pre-nuptial agreement. Mother comes too -?" Her pout was too much for him to resist. "OK. Mother comes too. And the vardo?"

With that the lights went out for John as she covered him and smothered him, so much so that they lost their hold on the sofa, ending up in a heap on the floor.

Before long the lounge carpet was replaced by a proper setting for love making, in John's bedroom. There they sealed their new promise to each other with a tenderness and passion that they had rarely reached since those early days together.

Afterwards they didn't talk, but simply lay there as the fading light filtered through the bay window to John's room. He later remembered they had the latest Van Morrison album on his record player, taking in the sounds without really listening. From that day onwards, whenever he heard *St Dominic's Preview*, he recaptured that moment and was transported back.

Although not by design the second track was called '*Gypsy*'. It was not his favourite on the album, apart from one verse that could have been written just for them. It took him back to when they would lay underneath the stars in the meadow next to the gypsy camp in Blaby, hidden only by the darkness.

All of a sudden they were sixteen again.

CHAPTER TWENTY

Funny how things always get in the way at the worst time

It had been a perfect weekend. John was driving Rose home at six o'clock on the Sunday evening, which was when they expected Sean to return Tilly, after one of her sleepovers. "You haven't changed your mind, have you?" As she said that she made sure she was looking straight at John so that she could read the answer in his face.

"Not a chance," said John. "If you had asked me seven years ago you would I would have given the same answer."

"I know. I'm sorry. So many wasted years... shall I tell Mum tonight?" She placed her hand on his as he pulled into the driveway.

"Why not? We should see what she says before telling Tilly, just so that we can see *how* she reacts. Not that I think she *will* react. Not badly, that is..." His thoughts then turned to Sean.

She was thinking the same. "Sean really likes you. He and I did part on good terms. I'm sure he will be OK about it, especially as he knows you won't affect his relationship with Tilly."

They half expected to see his car out front. Obviously Sean was running a little late. Otherwise Tilly would already have been down the stairs and skipping across the gravel to their car to meet Rose. They decided to wait in the Land Rover until the three of them arrived back. Mrs Lee had invited herself to spend the weekend with Sean and Tilly, just for a change.

John and Rose continued their discussion on how best to break their news – their good news – to them all. "I *will* have to tell Mum tonight, I won't be able to resist!" she was excited about it again, just the very idea. "If all goes well I will pick the best time next week to tell Tilly Then again, perhaps we wait until the end of the week when we're all together. She'll have the weekend for it to sink in."

"And Sean?" asked John.

"I'll talk to Mum first," she said. "We shouldn't wait too long after we tell Tilly, just in case she tells him first. Maybe I call him after work one evening, then it will be less of a shock.

rather than wait for his next weekend with Tilly. I know we've only been divorced for a few months but we did separate over two years ago. He must have been expecting something like this sooner or later."

Just then, car wheels crunching on gravel announced Sean returning with her precious cargo. "Mummy!" shouted Tilly as she ran up to Rose, arms outstretched.

She was out in a flash, catching Tilly as she launched herself, ready to be swung round before being lowered gently and gathered into a massive hug. "Gosh, you're heavy!" she said. "Has Daddy been feeding you those naughty 'burgers again?"

Sean grinned, guilty as charged, walking up to Rose to give her a kiss on the cheek before reaching for John's outstretched hand.

"Good to see you again," he said. "Keeping well?"

They had barely joined hands before there was an almighty "Crack!" drowning Sean's last words. John didn't hear it, slumping forward onto Sean before sliding to the gravel, lifeless. Rose screamed - blood oozed from a wound on the side of his head.

"Get down! All of you!" shouted Sean. "Behind the car!" With that he dragged John behind the Land Rover, keeping low. He had seen the flash out of the corner of his eye and over John's shoulder, from just over the high stone wall bordering the garden.

Rose was hysterical as she reached over to John. "Don't leave me! Don't leave me now!" panicked by John laying there motionless. "Not again!"

Sean stripped off his scarf, folding it quickly into a pad as he pressed it to the source of the bleeding. "Call 999, now!" he said, signalling to Mrs Lee to take Tilly inside but under the protection of the Land Rover. Sean was now on automatic, making John as comfortable as possible even though he was out cold. It was a head wound so there was naturally a lot of blood, but as far as he could see it was a graze, the bullet carrying on past Sean, luckily missing him by inches. "He should be OK," he said calmly, for his own sake as much as for Rose's. "The bastards were after me."

Rose was totally focused on John, but Sean's last remark

didn't escape her. "What do you mean?" she asked.

"I'll explain later," was all he could say. "Check to make sure your Mum has got through to the ambulance. I've got this."

Much to his surprise, Rose did exactly as she was told. She knew Sean had taken First Aid as part of his job, but was still impressed with how Sean had taken control of the situation. She, too, wanted to make sure help was on its way, and fast. Soon they heard the sound of the ambulance as it hit Mutley Plain at speed, before turning into the avenue and their drive a minute later. Paramedics sprang into action, relieving Sean so he could comfort Rose.

"I think we're lucky," said one of the ambulance men, "it looks like a graze. There's always a lot of blood but the wound looks clean enough. We'll get him to A&E, but we'll have to wait until he comes round before we can properly assess the damage."

"Can I come with you?" Rose broke away from Sean, making her way to get into the ambulance with John on a stretcher.

"You can't do anything, we'll follow on behind." Sean was saying this for the paramedics' benefit and agreement, as much as for Rose. The ambulance pulled away slowly, siren blaring, as Sean and Rose went up to Mrs Lee and Tilly. "He'll be OK."

"He's got to be," said Rose, softly, "I can't lose him a second time." Sean was puzzled by this last remark when it came back to him later, but right now it didn't register. He followed Rose to see how her mother and Tilly were coping. He was preoccupied by what had just happened. There were a lot of unanswered questions but right now there was just John to think about.

Mrs Lee did the only thing she could think of in a crisis. She made a pot of tea while they all sat round in the kitchen trying to make sense of the situation. Of course none of them could, apart from Sean, that is. But Sean didn't volunteer any information, nor did Rose press him for explanations. Just yet. Refusing a second cup of tea, Rose was eager to get to A&E to be by John's side. Sean offered to take her, duty mixed with a feeling of responsibility and guilt. Not that Rose was aware why. They arrived less than an hour after John's admission, and waited. He was in a coma.

CHAPTER TWENTY ONE

Something unexpected pulls John through

John awoke to find himself in a dense wood. By the angle of the sun it must have been late afternoon, the rays filtering through the branches and leaves, providing just enough warmth to be pleasant. It was summer and the scent of the honeysuckle was like a drug, made even more powerful due to the recent rain. The leaves above him were still surrendering their last droplets as he made his way towards a clearing.

It was the strength of the sun, the glare and light it emitted as its beams funnelled down on the grassy area in the midst of the trees, made it feel like a celebration. It was their voices that he heard first. Young mixed with old, but happy and chattering, calling out to each other. But not in anger. The darkness of the wood was in such sharp contrast to the blaze of light he encountered as he reached the edge. He couldn't see the figures whose voices he'd heard. Not at first.

Then a solitary figure slowly appeared before him, just a few yards away, but more distant from the other voices. It was his sister - Elizabeth. She was calling him, beckoning him to come out of the dark wood into the light, and join them. But join who? Gradually, the other figures became visible to him, out in the centre of the glade. They were loved ones he had not seen in such a long time – his family! There was his Mum and Dad, then his oldest sister, Marie and, finally Baz, his older brother. Running rings excitedly round and round the group were his two dogs – his short-haired collie cross Bess, and Bob, a long-haired collie cross. But something wasn't right. They were all so young!

For a start, neither of his two dogs were still alive, although it was a joy to see them playing together again. His brother could have been only eleven or so – not as he should be, in his twenties - and was holding onto his Mum's hand as they walked along. On the the other side, holding his Dad's hand, was Marie. She was still only just twenty he guessed.

But it was his Mum and Dad that held his attention most. They walked along casually just like a courting couple. He couldn't recall his mum ever going out without a hat on. Not in public. Now her hair was tied gently by a ribbon, blowing carelessly in the light breeze. His Dad, too, linking arms with John's Mum, wore a casual cardigan and cream slacks – just like he had seen in photographs he remembered. Old photographs – before he was born, and when his parents used to play tennis.

Elizabeth was so much younger too, only sixteen. And *all* their clothes – *so* old-fashioned. Then he looked down at himself, what *he* was wearing. True to life they were mainly hand-me-downs from Baz, clean but obviously already worn for some time by someone else and past their best. On his feet were boots, actual leather boots high up the ankle, with leather soles. Where were his trainers? He froze. He couldn't speak, let alone move.

Then Elizabeth took hold of his hand with a "Come on. Let's join the others. They've been waiting for you."

They skipped along the meadow until they reached the group, his family. His Mum turned to face him first. She knelt down so that her face was the same height as his. "John! Where have you been? We thought we'd lost you," she said, hugging him tight. She was *so* young, her grey hair replaced by dark brown, the same as his. Baz, whose hand she had let go just stood, watching, perhaps a little jealous of all the attention his little brother was getting. Then his Dad released *his* hold of Marie to kneel down next to his Mum, one arm around her, the other around him.

"We've been worried, son. You were gone such a long time. We waited and waited. So eventually we thought we'd take a stroll, all the family together." With that he wrapped his young son in both his arms, then, "Do you know where we are? It's Swithland Woods, your favourite place. We thought 'if he's going to come back at all, it'll be here'. And we were right. We *all* used to come here at weekends sometimes, when you were a little boy. Do you remember?"

John was still puzzled. He thought he *was* still a little boy. After all, they were all so young. And his dogs – alive again. He called them. "Bess, here girl. Bob, over here. It's me." They had been oblivious to the new arrival – him – at first then, breaking off from their game of chase they bounded up to him, jumping all over him licking his face. Theirs was the best welcome of all. Everyone started laughing at the spectacle, so happy to be reunited, all together once again.

It was Elizabeth who had saved him for the final hug, delight and relief spilling out as she covered his face with her tears. "There's someone else here to see you," she said. "Look over there."

With that, they both turned to see the lone figure appearing in the distance, out of the dark wood from where he had just come. As the figure came closer into the sunlight he could see that it was a girl. Young, but by now probably at least sixteen. But who could it be? The only people he knew when he was little were his family. Then he recognised her. It was Rose.

His sister spoke first, "John, now listen to me carefully. This is someone special you must always keep close to you. Share with her all your thoughts, all your dreams, and she will share hers with you. She will look after you as long as you look after her. If ever anything happens so that you cannot be together for a time, for whatever reason, keep her close and safe inside you. Let nothing come between you. Ever. Promise you will never lose faith in her."

With that Rose spoke. As he stood facing her, he suddenly realised they were the same height. He, too, was now sixteen, in his jeans and baseball boots. "Hello John," she said...

"John! John! Wake up John. It's me, Rose!" then to the nurse behind her, "He's waking up... John, can you hear me?"

"I could if you didn't shout so loud," he replied dozily, almost incoherent. Rose's face slowly came into focus, inches from his."Rose? Is that really you? Where's my Mum, Dad, my sisters and brother? Where am I?"

"You're in hospital. You've been hurt. Don't you remember? You were shot."

"Shot? Who by?"

"Let's not bother about that now," she said. "Nurse? Is the doctor on his way? John, how do you feel?"

"Like I've been shot in the head." They both laughed at this, but it hurt John, so he stopped with a groan. He looked up at her, "We must never leave each other again, do you hear, Rose?" His sister's words were still filtering through the haze.

Rose released his hand as the doctor hurried in to check on his patient. It was a Dr. Bruce.

"Can you wait outside for a moment, Mrs Ryan?" Rose left him to carry out his standard procedures for a patient recovering from a coma, deciding to call her Mum whilst she was waiting to be allowed back in by John's bedside.

It was the longest thirty minutes she could remember but she was relieved to see Dr. Bruce smiling as he emerged from John's private room. "So far the signs are positive," he said, but I do need to keep a close eye on him for the next forty eight hours. Head injuries can be tricky and you cannot really be certain what trauma has been suffered until any swelling goes down and the wound has healed. It's other parts of the brain that can be affected, not just where the injury occurred. The good thing is that his vision, hearing and speech seem to be intact, as well as his senses and reflexes in other parts of his body. You can stay for another half hour, but then I suggest you let him rest and get some sleep yourself. You look exhausted. Go home Mrs Ryan. I'm sure he'll be fine."

Rose returned to John's bedside but obeyed the doctor's last instructions soon after. She held his hand and attempted some conversation, but he was clearly under medication and found it difficult to stay awake, let alone talk. He fell asleep after half an hour and, feeling the need for sleep herself, she kissed him goodbye, promising to see him the next day.

With that he stirred, waking up briefly "Don't ever leave me again," he whispered as she left. She was close to tears making her way to her car but managed to hold herself together until she was in the driver's seat again. Uttering a massive sigh of relief and his last words ringing in her head, she made her way slowly home.

John's initial recovery period lasted just over a week. He was comfortable but he did have to take some tests and wait for the results, before he was allowed home. Thereafter it was to be a regime of taking it easy, with plenty of rest, and no stress or exertion. He would convalesce at Rose's for the time being to make sure he stuck to the rules, as well as having help near if he needed it. He did not object as it meant that he could share Rose's room with her. It also worked out well for another reason; Tilly would get used to John being around, and together with Rose sleeping in her room. During the day of course, he had a nurse on call in the form of Mrs Lee. She was only too pleased to have company while Rose was at work and Tilly at school. Would this be the ideal 'trial run'?

The one big question for which there was still no answer - so far - was 'why had John been shot in the first place?' John was adamant he didn't know and Rose believed him. Why shouldn't she? But the behaviour of the police had been a little strange. They questioned everyone immediately, including neighbours. For the first two days the area was cordoned off as a crime scene. They had to gather forensic evidence – shell casings, footprints, a record of any suspicious cars parked nearby, establish the trajectory of the bullet. And so on. The shot – a rifle shot – had come from the other side of a neighbouring garden wall. The owners were away at the time. But apparently it had not been a high powered, high velocity rifle. The distance was quite close range, for a rifle at least. But why had the shooter missed if it was such an easy target? It seemed amateurish at best; and bungled at worst.

Before the police left they also collected names of recent visitors, friends, and employers so that they could check out backgrounds and possibly identify key individuals for motive and opportunity. They seemed especially interested in their Romany and Irish connections, especially Sean. But after a short period maintaining police protection outside the flat, the detective team withdrew and left them to wonder and speculate on their own.

Because of the gun shot incident everything else had been 'on hold'. This included announcing they were planning to get married. The ideal time was soon to come when John was given the 'all clear' after a couple of weeks convalescence at the flat, and in the process of returning to his own place in Lipsom Vale. Mrs Lee was first on the list but she had already seen it coming. She loved the idea as long as she wasn't really 'losing' a daughter this time. When Rose and Sean had married they were initially in a gypsy camp, so Rose was always close by. Likewise, after they had moved to Plymouth, the family unit became stronger when the three of them, Rose, Tilly and Mrs Lee, lived together in the flat.

Tilly was a rather different affair because they did not want Sean's position as Tilly's real father to be affected. Luckily, the brief period of John living with them while he was getting better, while he and Rose were sleeping together, worked in their favour. Tilly had already seen how well Sean and John got on so any issues, whatever they could have been, never arose. All she wanted to know was that she was going to see Daddy as often as she had been. With that being a definite 'Yes' she was totally fine – even to the point of looking forward to the whole idea.

Then there was the question of Sean. As agreed before the incident, Rose had suggested that she call Sean first to broach the idea – certainly before he was due for his next weekend with Tilly. This she did, immediately after talking it through with Tilly. Sean's reaction was not the one she expected. He said he needed to talk to her urgently, to them both in fact, planning to meet them at the flat the next evening after work. Rose broke the news to John. They both spent the following twenty four hours turning over in their minds what could possibly be so vital that he had to come and see them. They were soon to find out.

Sean had left work early to beat the traffic for his run down from Exeter to Plymouth that afternoon. He wanted to spend some time with Tilly before she had to get ready for bed. He also relished the idea of one of his ex-mother in law's meals so he made sure he arrived in time for tea. Afterwards, and when Tilly was settled, Sean, Rose and John went to the bottom of the garden so they could sit in the summer house and talk in privacy and, hopefully, in safety. Over tea they had not discussed what they thought was the main reason for Sean's visit. Luckily Tilly did not raise the subject either.

Sean spoke first. "I'm so pleased for you both," he said. "It didn't come as a surprise, though." He shook John by the hand then reached across to kiss Rose on the cheek. "When do you think you'll tie the knot?"

"We haven't got that far, yet," said Rose, blushing and visibly relieved at Sean's positive reaction. "We wanted to tell you, Mum and Tilly first before making any arrangements. It's important that everyone is happy about it, and that includes you, Sean."

"That's right. Especially you. It means a lot to us both, Sean," agreed John. "But I must say we were a bit worried after Rose spoke to you yesterday, and you said you wanted to talk to us urgently."

"Sorry." Sean's expression changed from smiling to more serious. "It wasn't about your getting married. There's something else I need to get off my chest. It's about the shooting."

"The shooting? How does that affect you? You weren't involved, apart from virtually saving John's life." Then Rose remembered. She had heard Sean saying something like, 'the bastards were after me', whilst he was crouched over John, stemming the flow of blood from his head wound.

Sean explained. "The shooting wasn't some random event, and they weren't after John. They wanted me."

"What do you mean by 'they'? Who are 'they'?"

"They were probably freedom fighters. From Ireland. Keep this to yourself, and I mean it. I have been working under cover for the last few months. The military have been a bit nervous about the influx of Irish labour coming over to work. There are barracks in Exeter, the Marine training school at Lympstone, as well as Naval and Commando units in Plymouth. Not to mention the dockyard. Potentially they're all strategic targets for terrorist activity.

I guess you could say I was 'recruited' because I was one of those mainly responsible for employing Irish labour. They knew my origins were Irish, of course, but they felt I had been sufficiently 'anglicised' to be vetted and then trusted. My job has been to identify and monitor any unusual activities, and report back on any known troublemakers.

Naturally I couldn't say anything beforehand and I shouldn't be telling you this now, but I felt I owed you. We all have Tilly's safety to consider. I wanted you to know that she will be safe. You all will."

"That explains why the police seemed to drop the case after the initial few days." John was posing a question as much as making a statement. But it was something that had puzzled both he and Rose at the time.

"Exactly," said Sean. I know they were collecting names of

all your friends and family looking for leads. As soon as they fed 'Sean Ryan' into their intelligence, my link to military intelligence came up. I didn't hear anything from the police either, just a de-brief from the team I report to, confirming that the civilian police were closing the case."

"So we really do have nothing to worry about?" Rose asked.

"Not a thing," Sean replied. " They – the shooters - must have been low-ranking and not very good at their job, otherwise they could hardly have missed me. Sorry about that, John," he added. "Our intelligence have contacts inside the local 'cell' anyway, and have made it clear - to them - that they got the wrong man. Even they are unlikely to make the same mistake twice."

"But that must mean you're still a target, Sean?" It was Rose.

"That's what I need to talk to you about. Until the local cell is 'neutralised' I'm still at risk. There's a surveillance team out there as we speak, to ensure it's safe for me to speak to you now. But until it's all sorted I will have to stay away from you all. Can you explain this to Tilly for me? In ways she will understand, but without frightening her?" Sean was addressing them both as he said this. He was relying on John as much as Rose to make sure Tilly got through this OK. Then Sean could return to his regular visits.

"Sure thing." It was John who replied. "But if you have to disappear for a while you'd better sort it quick, otherwise you'll miss the wedding." They all laughed.

"I'll do my best," Sean said. "It might not be a bad idea for Rose to change her name from 'Ryan' sooner rather than later, anyway." They could see that he was half-serious. "But John, one more thing." Now Sean was being real serious. "I know you have Irish friends, really good Irish friends, so I know I can rely on you totally to keep all this away from them. It may be just a precaution, but I know what even the best of them can be like after a drink. I never suspected your Plymouth pals in any case. For one thing you're Protestant and they're Catholic. If they did have any issues with that then it would have shown by now. And, just so you know, they have all been thoroughly vetted. All came up 'clean'. In fact, as far as we know there is nobody in either site, Exeter or Plymouth, with any connections. But we still have to be careful."

Rose heard this too, nodding her agreement and approval. "We are so grateful to you, Sean, for trusting us. We won't let you down. Now I guess we'd better go back in or my Mum will be worried."

They made their way back into the house where Sean said his goodbyes to Mrs Lee and Tilly, before getting into his car to drive home. Of course, Mrs Lee was curious about the 'secret meeting' as she called it, but they brushed it off, explaining that Sean merely wanted assurances that Tilly would be well looked after, and that his access rights would continue. She appeared to accept it.

CHAPTER TWENTY TWO

A new life begins

Within two months of Sean revealing what was behind the shooting, John and Rose were on their way to St Ives for their honeymoon.

Their wedding went smoothly, if that's ever possible for 'the happiest day of your life'. As much as he could, John stayed out of the organising arrangements. They wanted a civil ceremony. Guests included Rose's friends from work but no family on her side, other than her Mum and Tilly, who was bridesmaid. John had his Mum and Dad over from the Isle of Wight – they stayed at John's - but his sister Marie was in mid-season at the guest house. Elizabeth was living abroad and unable to come at the relatively short notice.

Baz and his wife came down from Leicester. Melv was John's Best Man. He was already married to the childhood sweetheart he had met shortly after school, when John was at college. It was good to see his best friend again. It had been a few years since he had seen Melv but they had always kept in touch. Mainly by letter. John's night out with the boys before the wedding – with Ray, Bren and a few others – had passed without major incident.

Sean decided not to come to the wedding. It was mainly as a precaution. The cell of freedom fighters behind the shooting had been dealt with by the military, but only recently. His wedding present to them was that he felt that 'they could get on with the rest of their lives in peace'. Going forward they intended to buy a place in Plymouth with enough room for Mrs Lee to have her own space, and a place for the vardo. Meanwhile they would make do at the flat, with John giving up the house in Lipsom Vale. They quite fancied a new house on a new development in Goosewell. It was on a good bus route into town for Mrs Lee, the school in Plymstock had a good reputation, and it was bordering the countryside. They could buy off-plan and move in towards the end of the year.

The drive down through Cornwall was easy. It was towards

the end of the season after the schools had gone back, so traffic was light. Their perfect day was crowned by a bright sunny afternoon with the tree-lined parts of the route the perfect back-drop to the day. They had left the reception at the function suite at the top of Debenhams by late afternoon so they could book into the 4-Star St Ives Bay Hotel before dinner. He had requested a sea-view suite. He had left Melv and his wife to the mercies of Ray and Bren, but hoped he would be fine. He could usually hold his own in any company.

His Mum and Dad were no strangers to Rose and were pleased that they were together again. It took some explaining, of course, but they were delighted in meeting Mrs Lee again, and Tilly, even though John could not reveal she was their grandchild. Baz and his wife, Jinny, drove them all down to make it simple for his Mum and Dad. They had combined his wedding with a few days in the Isle of Wight at Marie's, just to make it a real family affair. The newly weds were contemplating all this and the rest of the day's events as they ignored the turn-off to Newquay. Rose broke the silence.

"So we did it!"

"Yes. Finally. So many things seemed to be getting in the way, but we overcame them all. Losing you seven years ago, then me moving away, finding you again, then me getting shot. We must have a guardian angel watching over us. "

"I think she's called 'Jessie'." she said. She caught hold of his hand and squeezed, gently. "Do you remember what we were talking about, the day you were shot?"

"About writing it all down, you mean?"

"Yes. We could start straight away. This week. It would give us something to do." He knew she would been hiding that cheeky grin of hers, so he didn't look over.

"You *are* joking, aren't you?" They both burst out laughing.

Soon they were past Camborne-Redruth and on to Hayle, before turning off the A30 towards Lelant, Carbis Bay and their final destination. Crossing the Hayle Causeway John noticed the new sea defences below the widened road that crossed the estuary. It was a new system recently introduced involving a 45 degree bank reinforced by ten foot square wire baskets filled with two-inch stone. John explained all this in some detail to Rose, again ignoring her grin and stifled giggle as she wondered at how he could suddenly switch to 'work mode', in spite of the occasion. As they descended the road beyond Tregenna Castle they were suddenly met by the idyllic sight of the small fishing village, bathed in early evening sunshine. They both held their breath in amazement, Rose wiping away the solitary tear with her left hand so that John would not notice.

"We're early, shall we go for a walk before dinner?"

Rose agreed. They parked out in front of the hotel while the porter took their luggage up to their room. John checked in then drove round the back to park. "We might as well grab a jumper and start our walk from here," said Rose. That was fine with John.

They were high enough to see the whole of the town spread before them, including the Island at the far end separating its own beach from Porthmeor Beach. "There's a nightclub over there, Mr Peggotty's, " said John. "I don't know what it's like but we can try it out." They carried along down the narrow streets until they reached Lifeboat Hill, where they turned right towards the harbour. They didn't really know how they had got there, they just decided to walk downhill until it levelled out. The wall to the right of the harbour was populated by hippies, complete with belongings, bedding and the odd dog. Plus a few guitars, some were actually being played.

"Looks like they've returned from one of the festivals up country," said John. They've become a bit of a permanent fixture much like the artists, until winter, when some of them go over to the Canary Islands."

"Or back to their Mum and Dad's in Manchester," quipped Rose.

"They still haven't started the re-build of The Lifeboat Inn," he said. "It's been a while since it burned down."

He wanted to show Rose St Ives because of his fond memories working the season, at their hotel. He also remembered many a lively evening there when he used to come down from Plymouth for a few days. It tended to be half term and holidays. He enjoyed the quiet so that he could revise for his exams. Even when he had been on work

experience at Peter Lundstrom he still had course work to
do. He figured there was no real point in going back to
Leicester and he didn't really know the Isle of Wight. St Ives
was the natural choice for a peaceful environment in which to
revise for his exams. His reward for a day's study was a few
drinks of an evening.

The Lifeboat was renowned as an informal 'job centre'
where seasonal workers could find work in the hotels. It was
where he found cheaper lodgings. There was a guy called Vic
who everybody seemed to know. He worked as a breakfast
chef in 'Mr Roberts', a boutique hotel but not able to offer
'live-in' accommodation to staff on site. He said there was a
spare room where he lodged at Mr and Mrs Dunn's on
Trelawney Avenue, just off The Stennack.

John was telling Rose the story as they headed for one of
his favourite pubs – The Sloop. "Vic was typical of many
seasonal workers, very happy-go-lucky. Ready to work hard,
but young enough to enjoy the limited time off you got as a
hotel worker, he fell in love with St Ives after his first holiday
here. One thing he said really made me laugh. He said, 'I used
to like my holidays. Two weeks away was just great, as long as
you manage just one "bunk-up".' Not that I agreed with him on
that point."

But Mrs Dunn was 'proper Cornish'. It was room only but, if
I timed it right about mid-afternoon when I nipped back to the
lodgings, she would sometimes call out to me, 'Fancy a cup 'o
tea and a piece of cake, John?' I would go through into the
front room and sit with her in the bay window overlooking
the town. It was west-facing and if the sun was just setting on
a glorious day she would say, ' The evenin' do 'ave crowned
the day, John.' I could hardly disagree, once I had mastered
her broad St Ives dialect."

"Sounds wonderful," said Rose, " but I hope you didn't pick
up any of Vic's bad habits. Or anything else he might pick up."

"Trust me," smiled John. He ducked his head as they
entered the door to The Sloop. It was just two small rooms so
it was always packed. Getting a seat was out of the question
even at that early hour, so they stood. Even that became
difficult *and* drink *and* have a conversation. The only other

option was to take their drinks outside, which they did. But that had its pitfalls too. Because of licensing rules they had to, literally, stand with their backs resting against the outside pub wall while they drank. "I don't miss this," said John, "shall we move on?"

Finishing their drinks, they doubled back but forked right onto Fore Street before turning right again into The Digey. It led to Porthmeor Beach which John was keen to show Rose. He smiled as they passed what was little more than an alley way, called 'Virgin Street'. What amused him was that it sported a 'No Entry' sign. *Was that intentional?* he wondered.

Surf was 'up' with plenty taking the opportunity of sizeable, consistent waves. The light on-shore breeze was refreshing if a little chill so they decided on a brisk pace, not only to keep warm but to make dinner in good time. Their earlier wedding 'breakfast' was already a distant memory. John resisted the temptation to point out Mr and Mrs Dunn's end terraced house by taking a more direct route by the side of the cemetery, over the back of town, towards The Terrace and their hotel.

They walked up the front steps and into the lobby to be greeted by the receptionist, a rather fey young man who they later learned was 'Glyn', sporting a surfer's blond hairstyle. He handed them their keys, seemingly paying more attention to John than to Rose. "Dinner is in half an hour, but no rush," he said, as they made their way to the first floor.

They took an hour...

Breakfast in this particular hotel was something John knew about, going back to the days when he used to be in charge of the Still Room. "The full English" was his speciality, topped by his excellent coffee (he had once been complimented on it by a famous TV star, Keith Barron, he was quick to tell Rose). To crown it all, he brewed every pot of tea using loose tea, not tea bags.

John was pleased to see they still employed a high percentage of waiters from the continent – Spanish and Italian. Rose agreed. "And so handsome!," she teased.

"What do you fancy today?" he asked, ignoring her taunt.

"I've never been to Land's End."

"OK," he agreed, "we can do Sennen Cove as well, then stop off in Penzance on the way back if you like."

It was a plan. They finished breakfast and were on the road by 9.30, to brilliant sunshine. They stuck to the A30 going down, making straight for Land's End. "It's so bleak," said Rose. "I thought there'd be more here."

True, there wasn't much there. Just a solitary hotel-cum-pub that was closed at the time. After the customary photo shoots next to signposts saying 'New York 3,000 miles' they decided to head for Sennen Cove. That was different altogether. Almost Caribbean.

They were one of just half a dozen cars parked so they had the beach virtually to themselves. The sun was now playing hide and seek in the clouds and there was quite a breeze as they walked along the beach. It only added to their sense of detachment from the rest of the world. Their 'oneness'. They stopped just short of the incoming tide, watching the surf crashing relentlessly on the shoreline, the wind in their faces. "This is more like it." Rose couldn't agree more.

"Do you realise something, John?"

"What?"

"This is the first time we have been away, to be really alone together," she said.

"Apart from the times *I* was alone. But I kept you with me inside," he replied.

"It was the same for me, John. Even though I had Tilly there was always a big part missing. It was like a massive empty space waiting for something, or for someone, to fill it. But you were never there.

Of course it was my fault in the first place, but I was so young. I wanted to look for you but that would have meant going against my parents. Not only that, the Romany life was the only one I knew. I didn't know *how* to look for you, let alone where. I knew you were going to college, but I didn't know which one.

Then of course I was married. I didn't love Sean, not in the way I loved you, but I did respect him. He treated me well even though he must have seen something was wrong. I think he put it down to early marriage nerves or something. After all, I hardly knew him, it was more like a joining of families. But I still felt *so* alone."

"That won't ever happen again."

"Promise."

They continued to the far headland before turning to walk back towards the car. The wind was slightly behind them now. "How about coffee in that little cafe over there?" said John.

"I think it's time, don't you?" she replied. "And it's your turn to pay." Joking, of course John went inside to order while Rose found seats and a table outside.

"Right,"he said, as he sat down with their coffees, "I'm taking you on a bit of a mystery tour next."

"Where to?"

"I think you've just missed the point." They both laughed.

They let their coffee last, relishing the fact they were the only ones sat there, contemplating the marvellous view out to sea, letting their inner thoughts take over.

Half an hour later they were on the way to...where? Rose didn't know and John made sure she couldn't guess by following the road map. All she knew was that it was about 20 minutes away. The back lanes were a welcome change from the A30, that much she did know. They had travelled inland, and east. Soon the south eastern horizon came into view as they neared the opposite coast. As they neared their final destination two opposite facing signposts gave them options, but neither helped Rose guess where they were. They chose 'Car Park', ignoring 'To the theatre', for now at least. The car park was empty.

"A theatre? Way out here? Are you kidding me?" she asked.

"Told you it was a mystery. Come on. It's only a short walk."

Rose knew they were in Porthcurno, but she had no idea it was the Minack Theatre they were going to see. The view from the cliff top was breathtaking. They could hear the waves breaking on the beach below but could not see it. Nor could they see the theatre until they walked down towards the signposted Box Office. "Wow!" That's all she could manage as her eyes swept across the terraced seats – a natural circular amphitheatre carved into the rocks. The Box Office was closed but there were leaflets on display.

"Dracula," said John.

"What?"

"Midnight performance. All week. Dracula."

"Oh," she said as the penny dropped. "Shall we book?"

"We can reserve tickets by phone. Back at the hotel." They walked back to the car with Penzance their next stop, about half an hour's drive.

"It'll be lunchtime soon. Fancy a bite when we get there?" He got her joke, but thought he might resist the temptation to laugh.

They didn't stay long in Penzance, just enough time for a ploughman's lunch in a local cafe before heading back to St Ives. By now it was mid-afternoon and the clouds had won the battle with the sun, leaving the day overcast. From his summers in St Ives John knew that the climate in St Ives could often differ dramatically from that in Penzance. You could set out from one town in brilliant sun to be met by a rainy drizzle or mist in the other. It worked both ways.

This time it was St Ives that blessed them with clear skies and a warm gentle breeze as they drove through Zennor, having taken the scenic route. John reminded her of John Betjeman's love for the village and St Senara's church. Soon they knew they were close to St Ives when they passed Osborne's Farm to their left heading into the town centre before forking right off The Stennack. They were driving towards their hotel with the town spread out before them to their left. It was straight out of the brochure, only better. It was another perfect day.

CHAPTER TWENTY THREE

The perfect honeymoon

It was a perfect honeymoon.

They travelled quite a bit using St Ives as their base. He pointed out all the places he had found when he spent the summers down there. It was also a journey of discovery for Rose, learning more about his 'between life' – the years between their break and getting together again. Typically she was curious about past girlfriends - without prying, of course, she would say! She was disappointed at the lack of drama and scandals in his tales, but glad that he had always respected his 'loves' (as she called them) and not just slept around to satisfy his own vanity.

"So you went out with Maggie twice then, over two years?" She was no fool when it came to picking on the detail. "You must have liked her? What happened?"

"That was my fault," he said. "The first year we got together at the end of the season and after a few weeks I had to go back to Southampton. She stayed on. We didn't even keep in touch. But she was like you in some ways, but not in looks. You're what? Five foot six you said?"

"Five foot five."

"Maggie was a couple of inches shorter, and with light brown – almost blond – hair. In curls. Not like yours. But she was slim and attractive, although her most endearing feature was her personality. A bit like yours," he quipped. She didn't laugh. "I remember one of the first times I took any notice of her. At the end of the evening I had to wash the floor around the two sinks I worked at. They were always awash and swimming anyway. And dangerous. People who had to use the rear entrance had to paddle through it.

Maggie was a chambermaid 'living in' at the time, so most evenings she and her friend would knock off earlier than us in the kitchen and be out of the door before we had finished. Often she had to step over my mop whilst I was clearing up.

One night she stopped, looked down at what I was doing, and just came out with 'Och! (she was Scottish) Are you washing Mr Floor's face?' I'll tell you, it just about floored me!"

"So that was it? A whole romance starting and ending with washing a floor?"

"No. I'm just saying how she had a quirky sense of humour and came out with outrageous things that made you laugh, or just think differently. We all used to go to the same pubs afterwards, after work that is. Which is where most of the back of house staff used to meet up, and after a while we sort of ended up going around together. We didn't get to *sleep* together, and it was just a lovely friendship."

"When did you meet her again?"

"Next season. Again at the St Ives Bay. But this time it was different."

"In what way?" she asked.

"I just went over the top. She started the season a few weeks earlier than me, by which time she had sort of hooked up with another guy in the kitchen, Pete. I say 'sort of' because he used to walk her back to the hotel most evenings when the pubs shut, but I couldn't say it was much more than that."

"You didn't steal her from him, did you?" She laughed.

"It didn't feel like that at the time. Maggie never said. This time we seemed – or at least I thought we were – at another stage of our relationship. Closer, more committed. More 'into' one another, each other's views and feelings, that sort of thing. It was more physical and sometimes I would stay over at her place, which she shared with another chambermaid. Ironically, her room mate was from Leicester. But looking back I was too intense."

"So you frightened her off."

"I must have. So she ended it. I was absolutely distraught. It was right out of the blue. That's how blind I was and I reacted close to how I had when you left. All that emotion must have flooded back. Luckily, in a way, I *had* to go back to college in a couple of week's time. Otherwise I couldn't have stayed around much longer, what with working in the same place and having the same friends."

"How long did it take to get over it?"

"Sooner than I expected, actually. Having to knuckle down

to the third year's course helped. Like the last time, I found it a perfect distraction. But there was another reason."

"Another reason?"

"Well, you know I mentioned the other guy, Pete?"

"Yes."

"He and I had become *such* good mates. We used to spend so much time together when I wasn't with Maggie. Part of the time she and I were on slightly different shifts. Pete and I had the same hours and this same wacky sense of humour. You know, where you both seem to see the same funny side of things, nobody else around you does. He was like a brother.

Anyway, soon after Maggie and I had split, she and Pete started to go around together. I think she was using him as a shield, not in a physical sense, more of an emotional one."

"That must have been hard from you. Did you lose Pete as a friend?"

"That's the strangest thing. In some ways we grew closer, even though I didn't see him much any more. The truth is, I was pleased for them both because I loved them both. That hadn't changed. I just had to keep out of their way to stop torturing myself."

Rose brought him closer so that she could kiss him. "That's why I love you so much. You believe in what's good and what's right, even when you're on the losing side."

Their favourite spot in St Ives was The Island, especially late evening. It was the best time to catch unforgettable sunsets, whilst watching the Portmeor Beach surf from a point just over the rise. The trick was to make sure the tide was coming in with a slight off-shore breeze. Then, if they positioned themselves at right angles to the waves, they could look down and across the line of breakers to spot the pattern of 'tubes' as they were forming.

Friday came, but way too soon. Their last day to catch the sunset. During the week they had been using their first real time together reflecting on what had led them up to this point, and where they might take their future. In many ways that was not too unusual a thing to happen on a honeymoon.

Back in the day, for instance in the case of Romany families where the bride and groom might not really know each other, the honeymoon was the first chance to get to know each other in *every* respect. That meant understanding everything about a person, much the same as they had been doing over the past week. Compared with most people, you could say they had hardly been back together five minutes before they decided to marry.

"You never did give me the full story of how you came to live in Mannamead Avenue, before I moved in," she said.

"Slice of luck, really," he explained. "The work experience opportunity at Peter Lundstrom came up at the end of the third year at Southampton, so I took it. It was a 'no-brainer'. The firm found me lodgings, sharing with other students. The tenure lasted from July, when the term ended, right through the summer, then – in my case – from that September to the following July. That's when my course ended. Southampton suggested that I transfer to the Plymouth department after my work experience, completing my final year of course work there.

The practical field work would be carried out under Peter Lundstrom anyway, so it all tied together. To cap it all, the company offered me a permanent post at the end of the course - with a proper salary plus management training, meaning I would still stay in Plymouth. That's when I made friends with Ray and Bren. Before I got the place in Lipsom they found me digs at theirs - the B&B on North Road West. When the course finished I had to move out of Mannamead Avenue in any event."

"And a few months later I moved into the flat upstairs," she added. "We only missed each other by a matter of weeks. How strange. But looking back it does explain one thing. Mum came out with the weirdest thing one night. She said, 'I sense John here.' She only came out with it the once, although she must have felt it more than the once. Soon after, Sean and I agreed to part and he moved up to Exeter. Luckily, we were able to hang onto the flat – in fact, I'm not sure Sean ever told the firm we had split up. "

"It must have been the Romany 'sixth sense'. It would have been even stranger if I was still there and you were still married," he said. He then told her all about the fun times he had with Ray and Bren, including meeting Victoria and then going out with Sue. It was a lot to take in and, by the time he had finished, it was getting close to dinnertime.

"We'd better get back if we want to wash and change for dinner," she said. "Then I can fill you in on what Tilly and I got up to."

CHAPTER TWENTY FOUR

The journey home – a new start – but will their past lives haunt them still?

It was Saturday morning as they sat having breakfast, looking out at the mist obliterating any chance of sunshine to see them off. "In a way I'm glad the weather has turned," he said. "If there were clear blue skies I would have booked us in for another week."

"Nice idea, but I am missing Tilly," she said. "Let's get going as soon as we finish this coffee." Their luggage was already in the car, so it was just a matter of checking out before heading home.

Rose did most of the talking as they drove back to Plymouth. She had promised to fill in all the missing years the night before, after dinner, but they were both too tired and decided on an early night - with *no* talking.

As it turned out her own account of their 'gap' years was shorter than she had promised. She omitted the part where she was married to Sean. She just felt uncomfortable covering those years, especially as he and Sean had recently started some kind of friendship. Instead, she spoke of her life at the office, becoming more social outside of her previous Romany life. She enthused about where her current job might lead. John didn't pressure her, knowing she would tell him about the early part of her marriage – and other moments - when she was ready.

But she did swear that she had no other relationships after Sean, until she met John again. In a way that explained why she and John had not bumped into each other, before their chance meeting just months earlier. During the time John had been out and about in the town over the past three years, excluding his spells in London and Teignmouth, Rose had been a virtual recluse.

"We'd better see about the completion date on our new house on Monday," she said, changing the subject entirely.

"I can do that, if you like," he said. "The site office isn't far from where I'll be working. I can do that at lunchtime."

They were looking forward to their brand new house – the first for both of them – spending the rest of the journey going over the plans each of them had for the 'brand new start'. They were so wrapped up in it all that, before they realised, they were crossing the Tamar Bridge. They had made good time and were only 15 minutes away from home. They guessed both Tilly and her grandma would be waiting for them. They had phoned just before leaving, with an estimate as to when they would get back to Plymouth. They weren't disappointed at their reception.

"Mummyyyyyyyy!." yelled Tilly as she skipped across the gravel path, arms outstretched to greet Rose.

"How's my big little princess," she asked, swinging Tilly round at least twice before letting her back down.

Mrs Lee went straight over to John first, "Good to see you home safe," she said, with a kiss on the cheek followed by a hug. Then it was Rose's turn for her mum's hugs. "We've missed you both."

The kettle was already half-boiled, so regulation cups of tea followed quickly after their arrival. John was carrying in their luggage as Mrs Lee handed round their cups. "You look nice and tanned," she said. The weather must have been better than here."

With that they launched into all they had been up to in their first ever full week on their own. Well, almost all. They passed round photographs of key places visited. Tilly was especially fascinated by the Minack Theatre and pictures of Dracula. Rose did have to allay her fears that he wasn't real, although when the strobe lighting was switched on and he flapped his cape, it did look as though he had been flying. Then it was Tilly's turn to show Rose her school work.

Once they had disappeared into Tilly's room, John sat in the kitchen with Mrs Lee. It gave her the chance to mention something very important. She wouldn't give him any detail right now, merely asking that he and Rose be dressed and ready by dawn, as there was something they all had to do together. Including Tilly.

Rose and Tilly returned to the kitchen half an hour later, but he decided to wait until they went to bed before telling her what her Mum had said.

CHAPTER TWENTY FIVE

Dawn came and they dressed quietly, itself strange in a way. They were all clearly awake, so why the hushed whispers? Then they understood why. Mrs Lee was already in the kitchen with Tilly, but she was unusually quiet. She then explained that Tilly had been placed in a trance, and that they were going across to the vardo. It stood there in the shade before the dawn light, across the lawn to the far wall, nestled underneath a twenty foot high willow tree.

The first blackbird soon started the dawn chorus in the half-light. It was so quiet they could even hear the gurgle of the narrow stream as it ran softly under the vardo next to it. As Mrs Lee had explained, pure running water was essential in providing her with the earth's natural energies. Rose understood all this. John was intrigued, almost unbelieving. Then he remembered the story about Mrs Lee feeling John's presence in the flat, even after he had left.

Mrs Lee reached the vardo first, opening the door and climbing the steps, creaking under their tread showing lack of use. She then indicated to Rose and John where to sit, whilst she lay the still silent Tilly in a cot at the rear of the cramped, twelve by eight foot area. She was now ready. Turning to John she reached for his hands, holding them both with the palms facing upwards, and began.

"John, you will be familiar with the seven year life cycle I should imagine? Just to explain, in most Western cultures it has been customary to celebrate the coming of age at twenty one. In the Jewish faith a young man goes through a process into manhood at age fourteen. In Romany and Celtic lore we mark the seventh year at each interval, but starting with age seven, for boys but also for girls. You will be aware that Tilly is coming up to that first transition very soon." Acknowledging his nod of approval, she continued.

"It's important that she enters this phase with a cleansed mind and soul. It's not purification of acts she may or may not have done, but more importantly of the acts of those around

Printed in Poland
by Amazon Fulfillment
Poland Sp. z o.o., Wrocław

63498782R00085